Wickingham Way

S.R. Grey

Wickingham Way (A Harbour Falls Mystery III)
Copyright © 2013 by S.R. Grey

Copy Editing: Amanda at Create Space
Cover Design by Damon at Damonza
Print and E-book Formatting: Benjamin at Damonza

ISBN-10: 0615912427 (print edition only)
ISBN-13: 978-0615912424 (print edition only)

Also by S. R. Grey

Harbour Falls

Willow Point

I Stand Before You

Prologue

The morning after the love of my life—the powerful and rich Adam Ward—confessed to just how dangerous the work he did really was he had to run down to his in-town office to pick up some business files. Not that I thought driving down to Harbour Falls was a danger in and of itself, but last night's revelations had left me feeling uneasy.

It was Saturday, so the day's plan was for Adam to work from my rented home (a lovely Victorian on the outskirts of Harbour Falls, owned by an equally lovely lady named Mrs. Heider). I should have felt calm and focused, but I did not.

I was currently sitting in Mrs. Heider's lovely home, penning my newest novel—a love story largely inspired by my several-month romance with Adam. And true, I was seated at a desk located in the turret section of the second-floor writing room, computer screen before me, but sadly, keeping an eye on the house next door had somehow taken precedence over writing.

The big Victorian I couldn't peel my eyes from belonged to Stowe Hannigan—Adam's one-time fiancée's brother. As Adam and I had only recently discovered, Stowe was also a hit man. *And* a member of the criminal organization my man was currently trying to bring down, with the backing of a covert branch of the US government.

I'd always known Adam's work demanded secrecy, as he designed and implemented sophisticated security software systems for domestic and international organizations. And I'd heard whispers early on that Adam was probably involved in some high intrigue–type liaisons. But I'd never really realized just how incredibly dangerous all that secrecy and covert stuff really could be.

Well, not until recently.

I tapped my fingers on the desk and sighed. Tangled webs and all that.

Concluding that my preoccupation with Stowe's place was distracting me from getting anything constructive accomplished in the realm of writing, I pretty much gave up and focused all my attention next door.

Cardboard moving boxes, which had been spread out all over Stowe's porch yesterday evening, were no longer in sight. Stowe was supposed to be leaving our sleepy little part of Maine—so where were those boxes?

Maybe the lack of moving clutter meant my assassin neighbor had loaded the boxes into a truck or something and would be taking off sooner rather than later. I certainly hoped so. Stowe living in the house next door, while Adam worked to destroy the organization he was a part of, hit just a little too close for comfort.

From what I could gather from my vantage point, there appeared to be no signs of outward activity at Stowe's house. Plus, his car was gone, leaving me to conclude that my neighbor was out. It was still early—and I'd not been up all that long since Adam had snuck off without waking me—but as I thought about it more and more, I realized I'd not seen any sign of Stowe, or his plain-white rental car, all morning…or yesterday evening.

Suddenly I had a brainstorm.

What an opportune time to take a little stroll next door and maybe peek in a window or two, just to see if Stowe really was all packed up. Maybe he'd already moved? Slipped out into the night, like the slippery character he had turned out to be. Maybe I'd find the house empty, which would leave me with one less thing to worry about.

I quickly saved the Word file I was working on—or not working on, as it were—and proceeded downstairs. I tugged on a pair of fashionable boots, zipped them up to my knees, and grabbed a lightweight jacket to throw on over my sweater. Three minutes later, I was standing out on Stowe's porch, staring into his dining room window.

Hmm…not gone yet, I glumly concluded.

There were way too many things in the cluttered room, indicating to me that Stowe was not even close to being moved out. In fact, from the look of things, it appeared my neighbor hadn't even started to pack up the dining room. Even more curious, the dining room itself didn't appear to be used for dining at all—at least not by Stowe Hannigan. The room was outfitted as more of a makeshift office of some sort, packed with a variety of home office–type equipment.

The heavy oak table in the center of the room stood covered in files, so much so that the dark wood surface wasn't even visible. There was also only one dining room chair in sight. It was wedged in at the far end of the table, facing what appeared to be a state-of-the-art desktop computer. On the floor, cables lay crisscrossed and tangled around the scattered boxes. Boxes that bore an uncanny resemblance to the ones I'd seen on the porch yesterday.

Oh no.

I squinted so I could better read the heavy, dark printing on the sides of the boxes. *Kitchen, bedroom, bathroom...* These were definitely the same boxes that had been out on the porch. So I had to question why Stowe would move the boxes back inside. The weather was good, dry for the past few days. Sure, that was an oddity for the northern coast of Maine at this time of year—but that was neither here nor there.

Perhaps Stowe had changed his mind about moving. If he had changed his mind, considering the circumstances, it seemed prudent to find out why. But to do so, I would need a better view. Unfortunately, the blinds on the inside of the window were only partially open. That meant from where I stood, I couldn't see what—if anything—was in the boxes. What little I could see, though, made it seem as if Stowe was in the process of *unpacking* his moving boxes.

But how could I be sure?

If I could just get in the house to check things out, then *I'd know for sure.*

I walked over to the front door and knocked, just to make absolutely certain my neighbor was definitely gone.

As expected, there was no answer. I breathed a little easier, glancing around to make sure I wasn't being watched. No neighbors were in sight, so I considered my options.

Hmm... I tapped my foot. I was looking at two possibilities. I could sneak inside, or I could go back over to my house and wait for Adam. Adam would want me to wait for him, no doubt. The only problem was I didn't expect him to return for at least another half an hour. And I was feeling too impatient to do nothing for the next thirty minutes or so. Consequently, I decided one tiny peek couldn't hurt.

With my decision made, I carefully tried the doorknob. *Locked, dammit.*

Hell if I was about to let one little obstacle like a locked door stop me. I was Maddy Fitch, best-selling author by trade but persistent investigator on my own time...even if my snooping and nosiness often bought me more trouble than not. But I was nothing if not determined, so I ran back over to my house.

I didn't use bobby pins, but I had a feeling my landlord, Mrs. Heider, just might. I raced up to the bathroom and dug around in the drawers of the vanity. Sure enough, I found a bunch of bobby pins in the back of the last drawer I yanked open.

Perfect!

Two minutes later, I was back out on Stowe's porch, prying open one of the hairpins and slipping it into the keyhole on the doorknob.

Okay, I'd seen this on TV, but damn, it was harder in real life.

But I was nothing if not determined, remember? And sure enough, after a few additional tries, I sprung the lock.

Yes!

I may have done a little victory dance, but then I remembered the neighbors. No need to attract unwanted attention.

I glanced around. No neighbors, no Stowe, no Adam. Cool. Everything was still quiet, so I turned around and stepped right into Stowe's house.

And then...I panicked.

Shit, what in God's name was I doing? Breaking and entering an assassin's home!? That was like entering a dragon's lair. Was I crazy? Even if Stowe didn't happen upon me—which he might—I knew Adam would kick my ass if he came back from his office earlier than expected and caught me over here. He wouldn't actually kick my ass, of course, but still.

Best he not find out, I thought as I hurried into the dining room. I was intent on determining whether Stowe's moving boxes were packed...or in the process of being unpacked. I hoped for the former as I hustled over to the many boxes and started going through each one as quickly as possible. Unfortunately, my initial fear was soon confirmed; Stowe was definitely in the process of *unpacking* his belongings.

Why, though?

Why would Stowe Hannigan remain here in Harbour Falls? Sure, he was originally from this tiny coastal town in Maine, and he had once had family here. His sister had been Chelsea Hannigan, Adam's one-time fiancée. But Chelsea had gone missing over four years ago, and his family had since moved far away.

Of course, events had brought Stowe back to town three months earlier, in November. Stowe had returned to retrieve his sister's remains after her body was discovered. Proud to say, I was the one who uncovered the clues that solved *that* particular mystery.

But the fact remained that Stowe's permanent residence was not in Maine. He lived in Florida. He had for the past decade, doing whatever underworld things one did when part of a multilayered criminal organization. Of course, Stowe wouldn't be doing much of anything criminally oriented for much longer if Adam and the government had their way.

And that got me thinking...

My eyes drifted to the numerous files covering the table. Checking a few couldn't hurt, right? It might even help. Maybe I'd be afforded some insight into my neighbor's plans for the near future. Information like that could potentially be very helpful to Adam.

Or so I reasoned.

In any case, without further ado, I stepped over to the dining room table and began to page through a bunch of random papers and files. I found nothing helpful at first glance, just bits and pieces of information on various individuals. Some of the files contained lengthy rap sheets. I assumed those were in reference to the assorted members of Stowe's organization, kind of like résumés for criminals.

Time was passing, but I continued to search and search. I knew I'd better hurry, though, as Stowe could return at any time. And if Adam came home and found me snooping—well, like I said before, that could actually turn out worse for me than Stowe happening upon me. Especially since I'd promised Adam I'd keep no more secrets from him. And this probably qualified as a secret. It was definitely sneaky at the very least.

With all that in mind, I hurriedly closed up the files I'd opened and stacked them back in the same way.

Or so I tried.

But wait...

Was the first file I picked up originally next to the printer on the table...or over by the computer? I held it up, frowned, pivoted left and right.

Still, I was confused.

Had I picked up the file I held in my hands from the empty space next to the computer? I couldn't remember. And I really didn't have time to figure it out.

Oh, whatever.

I stepped to my left and placed the file causing me so much concern on top of another file marked, "Reopened."

Curious as to what *reopened* meant, I flipped the file open so I could read the contents.

It was then and there I almost collapsed, right smack dab in the middle of Stowe's cluttered dining room floor.

All because of one piece of paper on top...and the five words printed on it that read: "Suspected project name— Wickingham Way."

No, no, no, no!

Wickingham Way was the code name of Adam's secret project to bring Stowe's criminal organization to its knees. This could prove disastrous.

The next page had a bit more information, just as damning.

Status of project: unknown

Recent activity: February 11–five offshore accounts frozen

Threat assessment level: raised from high to critical

Previous directive status: hold

Updated directive status: February 11– eliminate target

Okay, this was bad—really bad. Stowe knew the name of the project Adam was working on. Apparently whatever Adam was doing—for whatever government entity employing his services—it was working, as evidenced by the five frozen offshore accounts. I was sure that was what had bumped the threat level up from high to critical.

February 11 was yesterday, so this was all very recent. Maybe *this* was why Stowe was staying? But what did this *directive status* crap mean? And what did *eliminate target* mean? Who was the target?

I was afraid to find out.

There was a glossy eight-by-ten photograph behind the paper outlining the directive. With shaky fingers, I slipped it out. And the photo contained…an image of Adam leaving his Harbour Falls office. Yesterday, based on the suit he was wearing.

Oh Lord, Adam was the target. There was no doubt about it. Hell, it said right at the top of the picture, in the border: "Adam Ward—target."

My worst fear had just been confirmed. Stowe Hannigan was assigned to assassinate the man I loved.

I stared and stared at the photograph of Adam, thinking only one thing: *God, how will we ever get out of this terrible mess?*

Chapter One

Adam Ward. Some days the man just wowed me to pieces, so much so that I could barely think. And today was turning out to be one of those days.

I watched as my exceptionally handsome boyfriend slid out of his just-parked black Cadillac Escalade. Taking long, fluid strides, he approached where I stood on the front porch of my Harbour Falls Victorian rental. I'd just returned from Stowe's place next door, but for the moment, I was going to set aside all the issues we'd need to discuss—like the fact I'd just discovered there was a hit out on Adam. I'd address that disturbing news in a minute. Right now, I just wanted to appreciate all of Adam Ward's fine, fine attributes.

Adam had left early in the morning, long before I'd been up and about. But he'd made it known yesterday evening where his morning plans were taking him. He'd driven down to his Harbour Falls office space bright and early to pick up some paperwork. But it seemed he'd forgotten to mention he had also had a meeting of some sort. There was no other reason for Adam to be as impeccably attired as he was today.

As he closed in on the porch, I checked him out. Always something fun to do. Today, Adam had on a finely tailored black suit, cut to enhance his lean and sculpted body. He was also wearing a light blue dress shirt, perfectly shined shoes, and a cerulean blue tie that matched his eyes, eyes I knew could change from serene to stormy in an instant. Adam's jet-black hair looked slightly disheveled, as was often the case from his habit of raking his fingers through the silky strands when he was stressed.

I had to remind myself to take a breath. *Breathe, Maddy, breathe.* Adam looked impeccable, amazing, as always.

I smiled, but as the man with the mercurial moods started up the steps, I noted his eyes were somewhat stormy, troubled even. Adam could be moody. I knew this to be true, but I loved him dearly. And I always would, which meant I didn't want to lose him…ever.

Spurred by a sudden fear that I could indeed lose Adam, especially if Stowe had his way, I ran to my man and embraced him with all my strength. I felt a strong desire to touch him, hold him. I just wanted to be near him. Worry had made me needy, I supposed.

I trailed my hands along Adam's wide shoulders and played with the ends of the hair that was curling at the nape of his neck. "I love you," I murmured as I rose to my tiptoes and kissed him fully on the mouth.

"Wow," Adam murmured, laughing as I finally slowed my kiss and dropped back down to my normal height. "What a welcome, Maddy. Remind me to run down to my office every Saturday morning from now on if this is what I can expect when I return."

A playful smile tugged at the corners of his mouth, and his blue eyes twinkled as I toyed with the lapel of his suit jacket. Whatever had been bothering Adam when he'd first arrived had passed…at least for now.

"Did you have a meeting this morning?" I asked, glancing down at his suit and then back up to his face. "You look awfully nice for a paperwork run."

"I did have a meeting," Adam confirmed. And then in a more serious voice, he added, "Actually, my contact from Boston flew into town late last night and needed to meet with me as soon as possible."

My pulse quickened as everything I'd seen over in Stowe's dining room less than an hour earlier came rushing back to me. Maybe Adam already knew of the hit that was out on him? Adam's Boston contact was involved in the Wickingham Way project and might have flown in specifically to tell him just that. It made sense, as this contact had already proven to be quite a resource.

When we'd needed information on Stowe Hannigan—before we knew he was *so* much more than Chelsea's older brother—Adam's Boston contact had been the person to provide us with thorough and detailed reports on Stowe. I wondered now who this person was and what he or she looked like. I knew nothing about this individual. Adam had never even mentioned whether his contact was a man or a woman. But I had a feeling it was probably a guy. I wondered again why this Boston contact was even here in Harbour Falls. As far as I knew, all previous face-to-face contact had occurred down in Boston.

I thought it over and concluded that if the government had somehow discovered a hit had been taken out on Adam, then they probably ordered the contact to come here to warn him, possibly even to offer protection. So, yes, Adam's contact coming to Harbour Falls was starting to make some sense.

Still, I had so many questions, and of course, my own information to relay to Adam.

No more secrets. This was my new mantra. It was also a promise Adam and I had made to one another following the Willow Point debacle. So it went without saying…I knew I needed to tell Adam I'd broken into Stowe's home. I had to come clean. And then I needed to tell him all the details on the directive I'd discovered. Maybe Adam already knew of the orders, but if not…

"Adam," I blurted out, "we need to talk."

Adam quirked an eyebrow as he watched me shoot a glance over to Stowe's house. The assassin had not yet returned, but he'd no doubt be back soon.

Adam asked, "Is what you want to talk about in regard to Stowe Hannigan?"

I nodded, and Adam grimaced. He and Stowe were not exactly friends. In fact, they disliked one another quite a bit.

Adam cupped my elbow and gently guided me to the front door. "Come on, Maddy," he muttered. "I think we best move this conversation indoors."

Once Adam and I were in the house and settled on Mrs. Heider's floral-patterned living room sofa, I spilled the beans. Adam's face darkened considerably when I detailed how I'd broken into Stowe's home. But before he could chastise me, I hurriedly delved into all I had discovered.

"Stowe and his organization know what you're up to, Adam," I said, breathless as I came to the end of the tale of my morning adventure.

Adam frowned, and I hurriedly told him the rest of what was in the insidious file I'd found.

Reaching for his hand, I suddenly had an idea. "Maybe we should get out of Maine, Adam. Fly across the country." I shrugged. "I don't know. We could stay at my house in Los Angeles for a while. Lay low, so to speak. What do you think?"

My eyes searched his, but Adam's blues were as inscrutable as the tie they so perfectly matched. A beat or two passed, before Adam finally sighed and glanced down at my hand wrapped around his.

He flipped his hand over and pressed his palm to mine. "Maddy, I'm afraid these people would find us in LA in no time. They've been very thorough up to this point and I'm sure they know you and I are together." He interlocked his fingers with mine. "As a consequence, they've surely researched your background. They know where you lived before you came back to Harbour Falls. Organizations like this one have a way of uncovering everything when it comes to their enemies." He paused, and his eyes held mine meaningfully.

"And you're their enemy," I stated, though we both knew he was exactly that. Adam remained quiet, so I continued, "That means the people connected to you are in danger too. Like me, right?"

Adam nodded grimly.

Suddenly, an icy finger jabbed at my spine. "Oh my God, Adam, you don't think my father is in danger, do you?"

My dad, Mayor William V. Fitch, was the well-loved and highly respected mayor of Harbour Falls. It would be very easy for someone with ill intent to find him. Very easy.

I shuddered, and Adam drew me to him. "Madeleine, your father should be fine. I worry about you because you're with me all the time. But ultimately, it's me these people are after. I think we need to keep that in mind, keep things in perspective."

"You already knew, didn't you?" I leaned my face against his solid chest and breathed in the uniquely intoxicating scent of Adam Ward. "About the hit," I clarified. "Did your Boston contact tell you? Is that what the early-morning meeting was all about?"

Adam was silent so I glanced up at him. He nodded curtly as he gazed down at me.

Since I was me—and infinitely curious—I decided to press a little. "What's your contact's name?" I asked.

I didn't really expect an answer. However, I got one.

"Agent Lenehan," Adam replied.

"Hmm…"

I longed to delve further. I wanted to ask if this Agent Lenehan was a male or a female, but I felt it best not to push my luck and aggravate Adam. This morning had already been stressful enough.

So instead I asked, "What do we do next? Do you have a plan?"

Adam's blue eyes, stormy as the nearby sea, met my hazel gaze. "I do," he said coolly.

"And what would that be?" I mused.

"We're going back to Fade Island, Maddy."

"When?" I asked, surprised by this turn of events.

Adam's one-word answer: "Tonight."

*

Adam's sudden announcement left me little time to pack, but I somehow managed to gather up enough clothes and belongings to fill two large suitcases. With a good-natured chuckle, Adam helped me load the bags into the back of his Escalade, and then we drove down to the dock at Cove Beach.

Our original plan had been to move back to Fade Island in the spring, two months from now. But to be honest, even if it was under less-than-ideal circumstances, I was content to go back now.

I'd grown to love Fade Island, the remote piece of real estate Adam owned. The island was located several miles from the mainland, a rocky and rugged land mass, often shrouded in fog. Fade Island could be eerie at times but also romantic. After all, Adam had kissed me for the first time at the old lighthouse down on the southern tip of the island.

The southern tip of the island touched at the heavily forested east side, which had never been developed and remained virtually untouched. If one were to continue northward, one would next reach Adam's sprawling compound. Apart from the huge stone and wood contemporary home overlooking the sea, there was a small runway, a hangar that housed Adam's private jet, and a seldom-used hidden dock, next to a facility that housed Adam's collection of boats.

The western side of Fade Island was a bit livelier, although not this time of year. A strip of vibrantly painted shops lined the aptly named Main Street, which was located at the top of a steep grade leading up from the primary dock for the island. It was along Main Street that Nate and Helena Jackson ran a small café.

Well, Helena ran the café. Nate, Helena's husband and Adam's best friend since high school, had long ago been designated manager of Fade Island. And though Nate did indeed keep things running smoothly on the isle, I'd long ago come to discover Nate was more than just a manager. He was also Adam's trusted business associate.

Translation: Nate was deeply involved in Adam's covert affairs.

Therefore it came as no surprise when, after we disembarked from the ferry and got into the sleek black Range Rover that was kept on the island for tooling around in during the winter months, Adam quietly informed me we'd be stopping by the café before we headed up to his estate.

"I need to pick something up from Nate," he stated casually—a little too casually—as he turned the key in the ignition.

"Island business?" I cautiously ventured, well aware that whatever Adam was "picking up" in all likelihood wasn't anything remotely related to the island.

Adam shot me a sidelong glance, his chiseled profile highlighted by the ambient glow of the instrument panel. "Yeah, island business," he deadpanned in return.

"Maybe I'll stop in with you and say hi to Helena," I threw out.

I hadn't visited with my friend for a couple of days, and I kind of missed her. Helena and I had become friends early on during my stay on the island, but we'd grown exceptionally close during our ordeal at Willow Point. I pushed the images of Ron Mifflin, Helena's sinister stepdad—who'd had equally sinister plans for us—out of my head. Thank goodness Stowe had arrived when he had, or God knows what might have happened. Stowe had saved the day…as well as both my and Helena's asses.

I felt sad. It was odd to think Stowe Hannigan had been the one to save us. He'd been a friend—of sorts—at the time. In fact, Stowe and I had grown so close throughout the deep winter months that he'd once accompanied me on one of my fact-finding forays. Back when I was researching another mystery—one I became aware of after receiving a cryptic letter from Willow Point, the creepy asylum where a former best friend of mine still resided.

But those times with Stowe, when I'd thought of him as a friend, were best forgotten. Things had changed drastically. Stowe Hannigan was now the enemy.

"Maddy, have you even heard a single word I've been saying?" Adam snapped when he realized I wasn't listening.

"Um, I..." I twisted in my seat to face him. "I'm listening now."

Adam shook his head, and continued, "The café is closed for the day. Helena's isn't there. You can visit her tomorrow, if you like."

"If I like," I scoffed.

Adam sure was being bossy. But he often behaved like this when stressed. To be honest, I sort of liked his cocky, take-charge persona. Adam was controlling in many ways, but I had to say when it came right down to it, he actually let me get away with a lot. History had proven that to be true. So I had no room to complain. Because of this, I gave the gorgeous man next to me no argument. I remained quiet and lost in my thoughts as Adam pulled up to the curb and parked the SUV in front of the darkened café.

Once the engine quieted, Adam's tense posture relaxed. With a sigh, he leaned over the console and placed a soft peck on my cheek. "I'm sorry I was short with you," he whispered as he nuzzled his nose near my ear. "It's just been a crazy day."

I turned my head so I was facing him, and immediately his lips captured mine, his kiss expressing more heartfelt sentiment than any apologetic words ever could.

When we broke apart, Adam trailed a finger down my cheek and leaned his forehead to mine. "I'll only be a few minutes, okay?"

I nodded against him, and then he was gone.

True to his word, Adam spent no more than five minutes in the café. As he settled back into the driver's seat, I watched him closely. I was curious as to what kind of "island business" he'd had with Nate. As Adam snapped his seatbelt into place, his suit jacket gaped open just enough to reveal something that had absolutely not been there before—a handgun. And this particular firearm appeared to be much more formidable than the .38 I knew he kept in a locked desk drawer in his study at his house. I later found out the new gun was a .45 ACP, but at the time I thought it merely big, black, and scary.

Adam caught me staring, mouth open, before I had a chance to avert my eyes.

"Maddy…" His tone was one of warning.

I turned my head away and put my hand up in a placating manner. "I know, I know," I said. "Don't ask, right?"

Adam started the Range Rover and pulled away from the curb. "You got it," was his all-too-somber reply.

*

It was crazy, but as we drove the dark, winding road to Adam's compound, I realized I found the idea of my guy packing heat immensely exciting. Maybe I was drawn to the danger of it all?

Pfft. Of course I was.

And because of my excitement, I couldn't keep my hands off of Adam. I ran my palm along his solid thigh, before squeezing gently, relishing the feel of his muscles bunching beneath the smooth fabric of his suit pants, especially when he pressed the gas pedal to the floor.

"Maddy, if you keep that up," he warned, "we aren't going to make it to the house."

Despite his serious tone, Adam's voice was playful, as well as tinged with lust—and promise—as we raced into the night.

"The cottage is coming up. We could always stop there," I coyly suggested.

I was definitely up for a quickie; I was that turned on.

The cute Cotswold-styled cottage I'd stayed in following my arrival to the island back in September came into view as we rounded a bend.

"Are you sure?" Adam asked, shooting me a wicked grin that let me know he was most definitely "up" for the idea.

Feeling playful, I decided to check for sure.

I slid my hand way up Adam's thigh. He sucked in a breath as I squeezed his arousal.

"Yes," I breathed out, "I am definitely, definitely sure."

A few short minutes later, we were inside the cottage. Adam kissed me furiously as he backed me toward the living room, and in the direction of the sofa. I loved that his kisses felt urgent and desperate. It made me want him all the more.

When I felt the cushion's edge pressing at the backs of my knees, I broke away long enough to unzip and kick off my boots and heavy winter socks. Adam took the opportunity to remove his suit jacket. I reached out and ran my hands down his sides, my fingers brushing lightly over cold metal—the gun.

Adam's dress shirt was already untucked from our fumbling, so I focused my attention on undoing the buttons. Meanwhile, Adam freed the gun from where it was lodged in his waistband. He set it down on the coffee table with care.

The cottage interior was dark and cool, with a closed-up feel. But none of those things mattered. Neither Adam nor I made any move to turn on any lights—the bit of moonlight streaming through the windows provided sufficient illumination for what we planned to do—and the temperature didn't stay cool for long. We heated things up rapidly, breathing life into the cottage with our gasps and needy moans.

Adam reached down and cupped my jean-clad ass, rubbing and squeezing my flesh through the thin denim. Once I had Adam's shirt undone, I placed my palms flat against his smooth chest. *So warm...so strong.* He always felt so good. His pectoral muscles flexed beneath my fingers as I slid my hand across his chest, then down over his tight washboard abs. When I slipped a finger under the waistband of his slacks, his breathing quickened.

Adam adeptly popped the button on my jeans while I worked his belt free and undid his zipper. Impatient and filled with longing to touch *all* of Adam, I slipped my hand into his boxer briefs and stroked his hard length. Adam released a groan and pumped into my hand a few times, but then he got back to focusing on me, urging me to lift my arms so he could remove the sweater I was wearing. In seconds, pants, jeans, undergarments, everything fell to a pile on the floor, until we stood facing one another, naked.

Shit. The magnificence of Adam Ward's unclothed body never failed to amaze me. Even near darkness couldn't hide his trim and leanly muscled build—athletically toned legs, slim hips, muscular torso. I sighed and raised my eyes to his oh-so-handsome face. He didn't meet my gaze immediately, however. He was too busy raking his eyes appreciatively over my bare body.

I quivered and quaked, certain Adam would take me quickly and roughly, as he'd once done in the Victorian rental, the night he discovered Stowe had been over for dinner. Adam had been insanely jealous...and I'd loved every second of being the recipient of his wrath. Even though no jealously or need for possession colored this encounter, hunger and need still hung in the air.

But to my surprise, Adam, when he touched me again, was gentle. He nudged my body back onto the sofa, lifted my limbs this way and that, tenderly, until he was positioned between my legs.

I felt more-than-ready for Adam, so I wiggled and arched until I was in line with what I wanted. He pushed at my core, his engorged head parting my folds. Still, he made no move to thrust into me as I'd anticipated.

"Maddy, look at me," Adam urged when he saw me staring down to where I desperately wanted our bodies joined completely.

I glanced up, and Adam held my gaze as he smoothed unruly honey-brown strands of hair away from my face. "No matter what happens, you know I love you, right?"

Adam's voice was but a whisper, and a lump caught in my throat. *I could really lose this man*, I sadly thought.

I nodded and tried to reply, but when he noticed I was choking up, he covered my mouth with his. Adam kissed me deeply and thoroughly, until I was gasping for air.

"I love you," he told me again when he pulled back so I could breathe. "You're everything to me, Madeleine."

Adam kissed me before I could respond, his lips traveling down my neck and his mouth fastening to one of my breasts. Adam worked my nipple into his mouth, sucking and swirling his tongue artfully around the hardening pebble. I moved beneath him, still intent on maneuvering him inside. But his weight kept me from getting my way. When it came to sex, we played by Adam's rules.

His hands moved down to grasp and still my hips, while his mouth moved to my other breast. "Your tits are amazing," Adam rasped as he nipped at my flesh. "I could play here all night."

"So do," I rasped.

Teeth caught at my tender skin and pulled, making me gasp, in pleasure and the smallest hint of discomfort.

"Maddy," Adam chuckled, before he nipped his way down my stomach.

When he reached my core, his breaths, hot and heavy, rippled over my wetness. With adept fingers, Adam spread me. He touched my clit with his tongue, making me moan out a string of completely incoherent words.

"Is that good?" he asked smugly between lazy licks that set me further aflame.

I had no words; I was too caught up, too close. But surely the orgasm that wracked my body gave Adam the answer he sought. With waves of pleasure washing over me, Adam entered me. He moved slowly but plunged into me deeply. I loved how Adam moved when he was inside of me. So it was no surprise when I quickly fell over the precipice once again. Although this time, he came with me.

Afterward, as we lay exhausted and spent in each other's arms, I thought about what had initially drawn me to Adam, why I had fallen so hard for him, and why I physically hungered for his body so much.

It all came down to one thing—danger.

Adam was dangerous; he had been from the start. He was a powerful and mysterious man with changeable moods. And danger surrounded him. I suspected this would always be the case. At least to some extent. And I liked things this way. Someday I knew I might feel differently. But for right now, I reveled in the danger of life with Adam Ward.

Not that I didn't love him just for him. I loved Adam no matter what, danger or no. But it was like a bonus, this underlying excitement that existed in being with him. It drove me wild with lust. It consumed me at times, made me heady. My strong emotions had often led me to make rash decisions. Lord knows I had acted unwisely on more than one occasion.

For example, when I'd first arrived on the island, during the time I suspected Adam of wrongdoing in the disappearance of his fiancée, I didn't care if he'd committed a crime. *I. Did. Not. Care.* I still chose to spend time with him, no matter how bad things looked at the time.

And more recently, when Ami contacted me from Willow Point and I ended up discovering that Adam had been involved in some capacity in the cover-up of a murder, it didn't faze me. Not as it should have. Sure, I wasn't thrilled with what I'd discovered, but my desire to remain with Adam never wavered. Despite the fact that—for the second time in just a few weeks—I thought him capable of murder.

Maybe he was capable of inflicting harm like that if push came to shove. After all, death certainly seemed to surround him. But now Adam Ward himself was the target. And here we were, preparing to hunker down on the island in an effort to keep him safe. Once again, being around Adam was apt to be dangerous. Only this time it was because he was in the crosshairs of an assassin.

I didn't know what would happen.

Would Stowe really try to kill Adam? I wanted to believe Stowe had gotten to know me well enough that he wouldn't extinguish the love of my life so callously. But I knew that was just wishful thinking. Stowe was a professional, with a job to do. Feelings meant nothing; they were just collateral damage.

I twisted in my position on top of Adam and caught sight of the gun. I glanced at Adam, felt a stir of excitement, but tamped it down quickly when I realized he was asleep.

The only time Adam ever seemed vulnerable was when he was sleeping. With care, I lovingly brushed back a lock of raven hair that had fallen across his forehead. He stirred slightly, and I froze, not wanting to wake him. He needed this tranquil time.

When his breathing regulated, I watched as he slept peacefully. Eventually I laid my head down on his chest and felt my eyes flutter closed.

As I drifted off, I concluded two things: One, I did indeed thrive on danger. And two, I would do everything in my power to protect Adam, including kill if necessary.

I supposed I was becoming a danger in my own right.

Chapter Two

The next morning Max Cleary, Adam's personal security guy for when he spent time on Fade Island, met us out in front of Adam's large stone and wood contemporary home.

Adam and I had spent the night at my cottage, but we'd made it back to his compound in time to shower and eat breakfast. And now, just like before Max's arrival, a gloomy sky loomed above as the three of us walked along Adam's winding driveway that cut through the surrounding forest.

Max pointed this way and that, up into the towering pines, explaining the security precautions he'd put in place to keep his boss safe. Like most of the island, the land around Adam's compound was not only densely wooded but also crisscrossed with narrow dirt trails, many overgrown and impassable.

Shortly after my autumn arrival to the island, I'd embarked on an exploratory quest through these very same woods. Starting at my cottage, I'd followed a meandering trail that had led me northbound, high above the ocean, and directly to Adam's driveway, close to where the three of us now lingered.

"Over here, up there"—Max gestured to various pieces of electronic equipment, hidden somewhere up in the trees, as he spoke—"and over there, as well."

I looked up and squinted as Max chattered on. The small devices, even when pointed out, were barely visible. You'd have to know where they were to pick them out.

"Surveillance cameras as well as motion detectors?" Adam inquired, one eyebrow lifting as he turned to Max and awaited confirmation.

"Yes, sir," the hulking man replied as he ran a hand over his closely shorn brown hair.

Max had once frightened me, especially after he'd discovered me spying on Adam on the day of my fateful hike. I'd been so frightened that when he'd covered my mouth with his big hand, stifling my scream, I had fainted in his arms. Since then, however, I'd grown to care for the big security guy. Max was a gentle giant...but lethal when he needed to be. That fact had been made clear on the night Jennifer Weston had held me captive at the lighthouse. Jennifer had had every intention of killing me, but Max had shot and killed her before she could execute her sinister plan.

I shuddered at the memory from not so very long ago.

Adam, taking notice, put his arm around me. "Cold?" he inquired.

"Not really," I said. "Just a little freaked out with all this..." I raised my eyes and waved a hand at one of the electronic devices lodged up in a tree next to where we stood.

"I know, babe." Adam sighed. "And hopefully this won't go on for too long. As soon as we have more intel, we can apprehend whoever issued the directive."

Yeah, the directive to kill Adam, I thought. *Lovely.*

My stomach twisted. I didn't know what kind of "intel" Adam and the government needed exactly, but I prayed they'd find it quickly.

To end the uncomfortable conversation, I nodded and quietly murmured, "Okay."

Adam refocused on Max, and I continued to follow along as we made our way farther down the long driveway, in the direction of the main road. I questioned silently why Adam had even asked me to tag along.

But then I knew why.

Adam wanted me close to him at all times so he could protect me if need be. After all, the island wasn't fully secured just yet.

Max stopped at the next trail, this one hidden by a tangle of dried leaves left over from the fall season. I knew from the single time Adam had transported us in one of his speedboats—from the mainland to Fade Island—that this trail led down to a small, secluded dock, one for Adam's use only.

"This is of particular concern," Max began, nodding somberly to the trailhead. "The brush is so thick I'm afraid surveillance equipment allows us only a limited view of the dock area."

"What do you suggest?" Adam asked, his brow creasing with concern.

"I can keep an eye on it personally for the time being, but I'm afraid I have to recommend closing this dock down indefinitely. It's the safest option."

Adam frowned, and Max added, "We could always put additional manpower in place around this area, if that'd be more acceptable."

"I think that'd be wise," Adam responded. "But even so, go ahead and close this area down. Just wait until later today. Agent Lenehan is due to arrive in"—Adam checked his expensive watch—"less than an hour. We'll seal everything off after."

"Very well," Max replied.

I perked up, still focused on what Adam had just said. Agent Lenehan was coming to Fade Island? Great! I'd finally have the chance to meet the elusive Boston contact.

I wonder what he'll be like, I thought. I'd decided the agent was most definitely a man, so I wondered if he'd turn out to be a stuffy FBI bureaucrat. Or perhaps someone much more interesting, like a smooth James Bond secret agent type.

While I ran through the possibilities, Adam relayed to Max the details of the speedboat the agent was due to arrive in. "White, with a blue stripe down the side. The driver will be a male in his early twenties. Besides Agent Lenehan, there should be no other passengers."

"Got it," Max said. "Once they're cleared and docked, I'll escort them up to the house."

"Uh, just bring Agent Lenehan up," Adam said. "The driver is trained. Leave him to guard the boat. An extra set of eyes can't hurt until we get this island completely secured."

Adam then told Max he and I would be heading back to the house, where we'd wait in the study for the agent to arrive. Agent Lenehan was to be brought up to the house immediately following his arrival to meet with Adam...and apparently me. The two men spoke a moment more, before Adam and I started back toward the house.

Adam appeared preoccupied as we retraced our steps along the driveway, so we didn't talk much. But I was thrilled that I'd be sitting in on this upcoming clandestine meeting with the contact. I had to say, Adam was certainly staying true to his promise to keep me apprised of as much as possible when it came to his secretive work dealings.

It was still early in the day, but when we stepped into Adam's Old World-meets-modern-executive study, the usually cool and calm Mr. Ward walked straight over to the credenza under the large picture window with a view of the sea and poured himself two fingers of aged Scotch. I knew that meant Adam was stressing.

"Would you like one?" he asked, tilting his raised tumbler in my direction.

I shook my head. "No, thanks."

I sank down on one of the plush leather chairs facing Adam's ornately trimmed dark wooden desk. The expansive surface was as tidy as always. Adam wasn't a fan of clutter, in business or in life.

He passed behind my chair and gave my shoulder a light squeeze. "You holding up okay?" he asked.

"Shouldn't I be asking you that question?"

Adam chuckled and took a sip of his scotch. "I suspect I'll get through this unscathed, Madeleine. My concern lies more with you."

"What do you mean?"

Adam tipped the tumbler back and polished off what was left. "I'm going to do everything I can to make sure you remain safe. However, there are some things you aren't going to like. I need you to cooperate—"

"Of course," I interrupted.

How could Adam think I'd be anything less than cooperative? *Then again...*

"Madeleine," Adam warned as he set his tumbler down gingerly on the desk, "let me finish."

Adam's blues were as stormy as the churning ocean off in the distance. I rarely saw him *this* intense, and it certainly was intimidating. "Okay," I replied meekly.

Adam's gaze softened. "I know it's tough for you, Maddy, but you're going to have to allow me to make most of the decisions until this is all over. Agent Lenehan will be working closely with us, making suggestions. Suggestions that will ultimately keep us both out of danger. I need for you not to be jealous."

What? Now I was perplexed.

"Why would I be jealous of him?" I wondered out loud.

I swear I saw Adam smirk before he cleared his throat and said, "Uh, there's something I should mention about Agent Lenehan before—"

A loud knock on the study door interrupted Adam.

What had he been about to tell me about Agent Lenehan? Why would I be jealous of this person who'd be trying to keep us safe?

I couldn't imagine, but when Max walked in with the agent close on his heels, everything was made clear.

What the hell?!

Agent Lenehan wasn't anything close to a James Bond type and certainly not a stuffy bureaucrat. In fact, Agent Lenehan wasn't even a man, as I'd assumed.

Nope. The agent who worked closely with Adam all the time was a woman—a very beautiful woman. She was so stunning she could pass for a model. This woman, who appeared to be in her late twenties, was truly that pretty.

"Erin." Adam stood to greet the long-legged agent.

I checked *Erin* out more intently while she shook hands with Adam. Wavy strawberry-blond hair, eyes the color of liquid chocolate, a great body. Ugh, I was doomed.

Does she always wear such short skirts and low-cut blouses around Adam? I wondered.

I certainly hoped not. But then I remembered what Adam had just asked of me, so I tamped down the many pangs of jealousy hammering away at my self-confidence.

"You must be Maddy Fitch," Ms. Stunning said as she turned to me. "It's great to finally meet you."

"Yep," I muttered as I held out a shaky hand. "Maddy Fitch. That would be me."

"Adam has told me so much about you," Erin went on as she shook my hand firmly.

"Funny," I retorted, "Adam hasn't told me a single thing about y—"

Adam cleared his throat and shot me a chastising glare. *Oops.*

I smiled sweetly at Adam, and he rolled his eyes at me. Agent Lenehan took no notice of our exchange, or else she pretended not to see. She smoothed out her cream-colored blouse and dark gray pencil skirt, then sat down gracefully in the chair next to mine.

I guess my smile had turned to a frown, for as I compared my far-shorter legs, clad in boring old denim, to the agent's toned, silk stocking–wrapped limbs, I heard Adam clear his throat again…loudly.

I glanced up to find my man eyeing me warily. He appeared slightly aggravated—he knew me so well—but then he smiled resignedly.

I knew Adam loved me, but I couldn't deny what I felt. This woman made me feel inferior. I hated to think in such petty terms, but I couldn't help myself. Agent Erin Lenehan was the exact type of stunning beauty the powerful and successful Mr. Ward would have pursued in the past. Not to mention, Erin had the whole sexy secret agent thing going for her.

It nauseated me to picture her working closely with Adam, like they'd been doing for months. All hidden away down there in Boston, meeting in secrecy, the two of them rendezvousing in clandestine locations.

I knew I was overreacting, so I tried to push my disturbing thoughts away and focus on nothing in particular. It worked for the most part, as I was good at zoning out. Still, I caught bits and pieces of Adam and Erin's conversation. And to my surprise, as the meeting commenced, my silly fears were somewhat alleviated.

Adam behaved in a purely professional manner with Erin. His interplay with the pretty agent was all business. The two spoke of things I knew nothing about, technical elements regarding the Wickingham Way project that went *way* over my head. It was all pretty dry and boring computer-speak crap.

When Erin placed her briefcase on the desk and leaned forward to pop it open, I was sure Adam would take notice of her substantial cleavage right in front of his face. But his eyes remained averted. He glanced out the window, then at me. He caught me red-handed, side-eyeing Erin...and scowling.

The corner of Adam's mouth turned up in a grin, and even I had to snicker a little in recognition of my oh-so-obvious jealousy.

"Sorry," I mouthed to Adam.

He just shook his head once, chuckled, and then focused back on the papers Agent Lenehan was pulling from her briefcase and spreading out on the desk.

"Nate has made some great progress here," Erin said as she tapped at a sheet of paper filled with lines of complicated-looking computer syntax.

Adam picked up the page and peered at it closely. "Hmm, it looks like there's only one more code left to break. Once that's done, the final offshore account should be completely inaccessible to our enemy." Adam set the page down. "I'll work on it tonight."

The agent smiled. "We have this organization running, Ward," she said with confidence.

Adam smiled, smug himself. He had every right to be. It was largely his knowledge of how to hack into the most complicated computer systems that was crippling a previously untouchable organization. Damn, my man was good.

Suddenly, just as Adam was about to say something, a volley of shots rang out from the direction of the private dock.

"Maddy, get down," Adam yelled as he stood and withdrew the formidable firearm he'd gotten from Nate, the .45 ACP.

I froze as I turned in my chair. Agent Lenehan was still next to me, standing now and brandishing a gun of her own. When I remained frozen, she shoved me off the chair and to the floor. "Stay down," she hissed in my ear.

I knew she meant business, so I obeyed.

Silence descended, but only for about half a minute. As I pressed my cheek to the carpeting, more shots pierced the stillness. This time they came from closer, much closer, until suddenly the whole picture window above the credenza cracked and shattered into a million pieces. Shots peppered the spot where Adam had stood earlier, pouring Scotch. I raised my curled fist to my mouth and bit down hard to keep from screaming. But then another spray of bullets showered the study, the closest yet, and I did indeed scream, just as I covered my head with my arms.

A few quiet beats passed, before more gunfire erupted. This time, the reports came from inside the room. The sounds were so loud I covered my ears with my hands and squeezed my eyes closed. When I dared to look up and take a peek, the whole study was filled with smoke.

I blinked and caught sight of Erin. She was crouched down against the wall next to the window, firearm at the ready.

I started to panic. Where was Adam? Had he been hurt?

But then, from somewhere behind me, I heard him call out to Erin, "Now."

Agent Lenehan stood and shot three times out the window. A single shot rang out from outside, then nothing.

When I dared to glance over my shoulder, Adam was belly-down on the floor. He was fine—thank God—and trying to reach me. I scooted back slightly but stopped when he motioned for me not to move any farther.

Silence ensued. And the smell of gunpowder permeated the air, even though the smoke was clearing.

Adam glanced up at Erin, and she nodded.

I supposed their exchange meant everything was okay, since two seconds later Adam was beside me, picking glass out of my hair, and asking, "Are you all right, Maddy?" His strong hands ran over my shoulders and down my arms as I sat up. "You didn't get hit, did you?"

I shook my head. I was shaken but unharmed. Adam's arms encircled my small frame, and I trembled as he held me.

Many things happened in the following minutes.

Max returned to the study with news that the young agent Erin had come to the island with had been shot and killed. A lone assassin had breached the perimeter of Adam's compound, having arrived in a speedboat of his own. He'd quickly and efficiently taken out the driver of the boat Erin had arrived in before making his way up the trail and shooting into the study.

"Agent Lenehan and the driver must have been followed," Max stately gravely to Adam as he finished telling the story of what had transpired.

"That's impossible," Erin broke in. "I'm certain we were not followed."

I didn't know, but to me, Erin sounded *un*certain.

"What about the assassin?" Adam asked Max, his strong voice reverberating as I pressed in close to his hard chest.

"He got away," Max responded in a low voice.

"Did you see what the man looked like?" Adam asked.

I froze. What if the assassin was Stowe? It pained me to think Stowe would actually come to Fade Island to hunt Adam down like a damn animal. Would Stowe really be so cold and calculating? He'd always behaved so jovially around me. I thought of the yellow friendship roses he'd once given me. And also of how he'd helped when I'd needed a cohort to provide a distraction out at Fowler's Motel.

At the time I'd been trying to uncover a secret Adam was keeping, and Stowe had been so helpful, making my little undercover mission a resounding success. Not to mention, a little bit of fun. But all of those things had occurred before I'd seen what Stowe was capable of.

At Willow Point, Stowe had struck fear in the heart of Ron Mifflin, who was no slouch in the scary department himself. So, yeah...

I sighed as I listened to Max describe the assassin. "The guy was tall, had a muscular build. He was wearing dark attire and a black cap. It was fitted snugly over his head, but I could see dark blond hair extending out from under the cap."

Shit, the description fit Stowe Hannigan to a tee. The only detail Max was missing was Stowe's green eyes.

"Stowe," Adam muttered under his breath like a curse. He'd obviously come to the same conclusion.

"Perhaps not," Erin said slowly.

Huh?

Adam and Max looked at her quizzically, but she turned her head away and said nothing further.

Hmm, interesting.

Why would Erin suspect someone other than Stowe? Especially when the description so closely matched his? Were there multiple assassins gunning (literally) for Adam?

With that horrendous thought in mind, I closed my eyes and suppressed a sob.

Before Adam had a chance to ask her for elaboration, Erin said, "We've run out of options here. I think it's time we move to plan B."

Adam exhaled heavily and murmured an assent.

"What's plan B?" I asked as I opened my eyes and stared up at a disheveled but still somehow amazingly attractive Adam Ward.

He sighed as his eyes met mine. "Fade Island has been compromised, Maddy. Our only option now is to hole up in a safe house."

Chapter Three

Not surprisingly, the safe house turned out to be owned by Adam.

He showed me pictures before we left Fade Island. We'd be staying in what appeared to be a rustic cabin, surprisingly modest in size, but very posh. It was located deep in the woods of Maine.

We wasted no time hanging around Fade Island. The day after what Adam and Erin termed "the security breach," we headed out.

Erin volunteered—or perhaps she'd been assigned—to drive us to our new location. Once we were back over on the mainland, we piled our luggage into her government-issued, nondescript sedan. Adam slid into the passenger seat, so I was relegated to the backseat. As we drove deeper and deeper into the heart of Maine, even from my limited vantage point, I had to say Erin's driving was impressive. The agent navigated the curving and slick inland roads with practiced ease.

Nobody spoke much. Adam worked on his tablet and I stared out the side window, observing the mostly white landscape.

Where we lived along the coast—and also out on Fade Island—most of the snow had melted. But here in the Maine wilderness, winter appeared to still be in full force.

Consequently, it took us hours to reach the safe house.

When we hit a white-out and Erin slowed, but kept the car moving, Adam asked, "Where'd you learn to drive in conditions like these, Erin? Was winter driving part of your training with the feds?"

Agent Lenehan laughed and shook her head, her strawberry-blonde waves bouncing. "No, no special training. I'm originally from rural Massachusetts, so I got lots of practice growing up. Driving on wintry back roads is like second nature to me."

"Well, I am impressed," Adam said as he powered down his tablet.

Oh, please, I thought.

The last few miles dragged, as the roads became particularly treacherous in the higher elevations. But we eventually reached our destination safe and intact.

Five seconds after Erin parked, all three of us were out of the car, stretching our legs and taking in the surroundings.

Wow, we were truly in the middle of nowhere. Everywhere I turned there was nothing but snow-blanketed utter wilderness.

Erin was wearing a fashionable pant suit with heels. I, on the other hand, had dressed appropriately. I had on high winter boots, jeans, a heavy coat, and a scarf.

I looked at Erin and nodded to her pumps. "Maybe driving in winter conditions is second nature to you, but I'm thinking walking in winter conditions might pose a challenge for you in shoes like that."

"Maddy, be nice," Adam said under his breath as he leaned in close to me.

Erin gave me a sweet smile as she held onto the side of the car and navigated her way to the back. She popped open the trunk and took out a heavy-duty pair of winter boots. They looked even more suited for the perilous conditions than the ones I was wearing.

"Don't underestimate me, Maddy," she said, smiling still as she stood on one leg and quickly swapped out a pump for one of the winter boots.

Adam rolled his eyes at our catty exchange. He grabbed a few of the heavier pieces of luggage from the trunk and headed toward the house. Erin finished switching her shoes, then tossed a small satchel my way. I just barely caught it, and she snickered as she brushed past me, carrying a large suitcase.

I was so glad Erin would be leaving us soon.

Once everything was unloaded and inside the cabin, as we stood just inside the doorway, Erin asked Adam if he needed anything before she took off.

"No, I think we're good. I had the place stocked a few days ago in anticipation of something like this."

"Good thinking," Erin replied.

I opened the door and stepped out onto the snow-covered porch. "Okay, then, Erin. You probably better get going. It would suck to drive back in the dark."

It was already late in the day and I couldn't wait for her to go.

She nodded. "Yes, of course."

Several minutes later, Adam and I watched from the porch as the agent drove off into the bleak white and gray landscape. Now we were truly alone and essentially stranded since we had no transportation at the safe house. I had balked at that decision, but Erin had insisted it was prudent for us not to retain a vehicle for personal use. Not only was there really no place to go out here, but the agent had claimed our location could feasibly be discovered by someone capable of compromising GPS technology. I'd expected Adam to argue with his remarkably pretty Boston contact on that point, but he had not. So I was inclined to assume what she'd said was the truth.

"What do we do now?" I asked as Adam hoisted up the last suitcase, one that belonged to me that had been left out on the porch.

"We'll figure it out," Adam replied nonchalantly as he turned toward the front door.

I followed him into the cabin. I hadn't really taken a good look around when we'd been bringing in the luggage, so I did so now.

The central room in which Adam placed the suitcase was large and spacious, like a giant living room. There were photographs of autumn scenes on the cedar walls, plush area rugs covered the hardwood floors, and the furniture was all dark wood. The sofa was covered in supple leather, the ceilings high and beam-covered. And across from the front door a staircase curved up the wall, spilling out at the top to an open walkway. Some of the doors to the second-floor bedrooms were visible from where I stood.

"Do you like it?" Adam asked, his arms crossed as he watched me take it all in.

I spun in a circle. "I do. It's very open, but cozy at the same time."

The cabin was well-lit but only because Adam had turned on several lamps. Not that there weren't numerous windows. There were many, but every last one had been blacked out with heavy partitions.

Adam frowned at the covered windows when he noticed me looking at them. "It's for safety reasons," he said.

I nodded. "I figured as much."

I supposed before the seriousness of why we were here could bring me down, Adam turned to me and said suggestively, "So, Maddy, now that we're here alone, what do you say we start a fire?" He tilted his head toward the huge stone fireplace covering one entire wall of the great room while his mischievous blue eyes remained on me. "We could maybe even open a bottle of wine?"

"Is your plan to distract me with sex?"

He quirked an eyebrow. "Will it work?"

I couldn't help but smile. "It just might."

Adam watched me carefully, and then said, "You don't even realize what today is, do you?"

I wracked my brain, but could think of nothing. "What is it?" I asked.

Adam fake-gasped. "Maddy, it's Valentine's Day. I can't believe you, lover of all things romantic, forgot."

"Oops," I uttered, laughing. With everything going on, I *had* completely forgotten about the holiday.

But now that Adam had reminded me...

"Hmm," I murmured, envisioning a nice romantic evening, just me and my love. "The fire and a nice bottle of wine do sound nice."

Maybe a Valentine's Day in seclusion won't be so bad, after all.

"I'd like to get cleaned up first." I smiled coyly. "But I can be really quick."

Adam chuckled and glanced down at the bag he'd just carried in. "This suitcase is yours. It feels pretty heavy, so it probably has enough of the stuff you'll need to get ready in it." He hoisted the large piece of luggage up with ease and headed to the stairs. "Let's go upstairs and I'll show you the bedroom we'll be staying in while we're here. There's an adjoined bathroom. You can freshen up in there."

Once we were upstairs and in the master bedroom, Adam plopped the bag down in the middle of a large king-sized bed. A bed I was sure we'd soon christen.

With that thought in mind, I smiled at Adam. "This room is perfect."

The room was quite nice, having the same rustic feel as the rest of the cabin. The walls were cedar, the colors complementary. But what I loved was that instead of large photographs on the walls, like downstairs, there were book-cases built right into the walls. And they spanned from floor to ceiling. Better still, the shelves were overflowing with novels.

Adam watched as I made a beeline to the bookcases. "Ah, I knew you'd check those out first thing. That's why I was sure this particular bedroom would be the best."

"Thank you." I turned to Adam and smiled in gratitude. Then I returned my attention to the books.

As I skimmed my fingertips along the spines, I noted Adam certainly had an eclectic mix of titles—timeless classics, modern-day literature, books of poetry, nonfiction titles.

"Wow," I whispered.

To say I was impressed would have been an understatement.

Adam strode over to where I stood and diverted my attention from the books with a lingering kiss to my cheek. After he quietly informed me he was going back downstairs to get the fire started, I replied, "Sure, great. I'll be down in a few minutes."

Adam left, and I spent a moment more with the books, before stepping back over to the big bed and opening the suitcase Adam had placed on the covers. I rummaged through all the clothes I'd brought, unsure of what to change into.

Ultimately, I decided on a simple long-sleeved tee and a fresh pair of jeans. Adam was dressed comfortably in jeans and a knit pullover, so my choice of outfit seemed appropriate.

While I showered, I thought about how this stay at the cabin might unfold. I liked the idea of having Adam all to myself. Back in Harbour Falls—and on Fade Island, even—Adam was often pulled away by business. Not that there wouldn't be work for him to attend to here—the Wickingham Way project remained his top priority—but at least no extraneous works concerns would intrude on my time with him. Except for Erin, who, I'd been informed on the way to the safe house, would be visiting us like clockwork every Friday.

Adam had brought a laptop and a tablet to work on, but we'd have no Internet service and no cell service either. Too easy to track, Adam had told me when I'd asked why we'd be living without these seeming necessities during our stay out in the woods.

Our only outside contact would be with Erin, through her weekly visits. Adam planned to work on the Wickingham Way project daily, and then upload his files to a flash drive, which Agent Lenehan would pick up every Friday.

I'd brought my own laptop so I could work on my novel, but Adam had made it clear I was not to communicate with anyone. Not even Katie, my agent and best friend out in California. Well, with no cell and no Internet, I couldn't contact her even if I wanted.

Not that I really even did. I was content with this arrangement. Adam told me before we'd left Harbour Falls that there were board games in the cabin.

"We can play some of those old games," Adam had said. "And when we tire of board games, there are tons of novels to read."

Well, I hadn't seen the games yet, but Adam sure hadn't been kidding about the novels.

"Plus, we'll have wine and nights by the fire," I reminded myself, smiling and thinking of the evening ahead as I stepped out of the shower and wrapped my dripping-wet body in a thick towel.

After I was dressed, I started down the stairs...but was stopped short by the scene below.

Oh, my.

Romance was definitely on Adam's mind tonight. Not only was there a raging fire in the stone fireplace, but a very nude Mr. Ward was waiting for me, stretched out on a plush area rug in front of the fireplace, wine glass in hand.

I sighed, contented and already aroused by the sight of Adam's naked body. The amber glow cast by the fire left some parts of him shadowed, mostly his lower half, but the muscles in his arms, shoulders, and chest moved enticingly as he shifted to watch my approach.

Yeah, spending this night in a cozy cabin in the isolated woods of Maine with the gorgeous and sexy Adam Ward had the makings for this to be my best Valentine's Day ever.

*

Valentine's Day turned out as great as I'd expected. After a night filled with hours of love, I felt so close to Adam. But to my surprise, it was during the days that followed that we really grew close.

Adam and I created a wonderful and romantic memory the first night, and to my delight, the trend continued as the first week wore on. I had to say, I learned more about the man I'd crushed on since high school—over ten years ago—than I ever would have had we, say, spent a year together under normal circumstances. But here, removed from civilization as we were, everything was heightened, in many, many ways.

For one thing, every emotion felt more intense. I guessed it was because we had no choice but to deal with one another, be it good or bad. Thankfully, most all of the time we spent together was good.

When Adam wasn't working on the Wickingham Way project, he spent his time with me. I'd originally feared that Adam would prefer time alone when not busy with the Wickingham Way project. But that was not the case.

The first few days at the cabin we took turns preparing dinner. Adam was as good a cook as I, maybe better. I'd discovered that fun fact months earlier. So it was no surprise when Adam wowed me throughout the week with entrees such as chateaubriand and coquille. I, on the other hand, stuck with far simpler dishes—hot dogs on one day, tuna noodle casserole on another.

Adam, thoughtful as he was, sweetly proclaimed my tuna noodle casserole to be "top-notch."

One evening after dinner, while scrubbing pots and pans at the sink, Adam and I got into a suds and water battle. I surmised it was Adam's thinly veiled attempt to fulfill a fantasy of seeing me in a wet T-shirt, something he'd once confided in me. When I told him I suspected as much, he didn't deny it. In fact, he encouraged me to take off my bra, but leave on the thin, white tee I was wearing.

Typical male, I thought.

But I didn't mind. Adam was best when he was fun. And fun it was. Ten minutes after we both were thoroughly soaked—me in particular—Adam was pounding into me on the slippery, wet linoleum kitchen floor. I had left on nothing but the tee, and Adam palmed my breasts through the sopping cotton as they bounced with every frenzied thrust.

And so the days went by...

Adam and I played, maybe bickered a little, but mostly we fell deeper in love.

Frequent and heavy snowstorms pummeled the area throughout that first week of our stay, so we had little choice but to remain holed up in the cabin. We often found solace by relaxing in the great room, usually with a roaring fire—courtesy of Adam's fine fire-making skills—crackling away in the background.

Since there was no cable, and thus no viewable TV, Adam and I read together quite a bit. We slowly began working our way through Adam's vast collection of books. During those days, as I'd lay with my head on one end of the plushy sofa, with Adam stretched out across the opposite side, our legs intertwined, I couldn't imagine life getting much better.

One afternoon, as especially fierce winds battered the covered windows—making them shake and rattle like nobody's business—I plopped down on the sofa, a book of poetry in my hand. Adam, all comfortable at the other end, was perusing some title on military history.

How boring, I thought.

I didn't know for sure if his book was boring, but come on.

I must not have been too far off the mark, as Adam didn't seem to mind at all the many times I interrupted him so I could share various passages of poetry that moved me.

After about the tenth interruption, Adam tossed his military history book to the coffee table and declared, "I give up."

At first I thought I'd angered him, but then he smiled.

We ended up sitting, shoulders pressed together, with Adam reciting the passages I most adored back to me.

"I love you, Maddy," he said after finishing one particularly stirring verse.

I murmured the sentiment in return, and then we kissed until our lips grew swollen.

When we finally resumed our respective readings, Adam decided it was time to share *his* book with *me*. Yep, the one outlining military history. I think he did it to get a laugh, or possibly to bore me to tears. Whatever his motivation, he opened the book and proceeded to point to a multitude of military weapons, giving me his take on each one.

My eyes glazed over as I tried to listen to his opinions on cannons used during the Civil War. When I could take no more, though, I stifled a yawn.

"Am I boring you?" Adam asked, his tone mock offended.

The man knew full well I had no interest in military weapons crap.

"No, no, not at all..." I waved my hand at some illustration of a cannon. "Do continue."

My smartass response earned me a thorough tickling, and that, of course, led to more kissing. Adam pressed me down into the cushions, his hot mouth devouring mine. But this time we kept on going. Needless to say, poetry and military history were forgotten that day.

Though most days went smoothly, Adam and I did have some spats. One arose on a Friday afternoon. I was feeling especially restless as the first weekend alone drew near. A large storm had dumped yet another foot of snow on an already thickly blanketed landscape. Agent Lenehan still somehow made it out to the cabin, but she stayed only long enough to pick up the flash drive with the updated Wickingham Way files.

And then she was gone.

I stood at the front door after she'd driven away, making no attempt to close it. "I'm so sick of snow. Enough already," I bitched to Adam, who was reclined on the sofa.

"Madeleine, close the door," he chastised distractedly, barely looking up from his laptop. "You're letting all the cold air in."

"Sorry," I muttered as I slammed the door, shutting us back into our own little world.

Most days I welcomed being locked away with Adam, but this day it irked me to no end.

"What's wrong with you?" Adam asked as he set his laptop on the coffee table. He'd finally given up on his work.

Truthfully, I was itching for a fight, feeling stir crazy from having been housebound all damn week. "Nothing," I mumbled as I made my way over to the sofa.

I perched on the edge, and Adam sat up straighter. "Quit acting like a child, Madeleine," he sniped.

It seemed Adam was in a foul mood as well.

"Quit treating me like one," I shot back.

A few choice words ensued on both our parts. But after Adam made a rather biting comment about how he'd rather be taking his chances in Harbour Falls than be stuck in the cabin another day with me, I choked back a sob.

Adam sighed and raked his fingers through dark hair that was in need of a trim. "I didn't mean that," he murmured.

But it was too late; his comment had already damaged. I stared down at my hands in my lap, at a loss for words.

In a soft voice, Adam said, "Come here, Maddy." He patted the spot next to him and arched an eyebrow. "Please," he added when I made no attempt to move.

I hesitantly slid down to the cushions.

"I'm sorry," he whispered as he placed his hand on my knee. "I don't want to fight with you, baby."

I blew out a breath. "I know, and I don't want to fight with you, either." I didn't—not anymore.

I curled up in Adam's arms and he rested his chin against the top of my head. "Are you getting sick of me already?" he whispered into my hair.

"No, not at all," I assured him.

When he didn't reply, I sat up and met his deep blue eyes, so clear today, so serene. Even with the Wickingham Way project proceeding along—and Adam still marked for assassination—I'd never really seen him so at peace, despite our minor disagreement. I had to admit this time away was good for him.

Adam tucked a strand of hair behind my ear. "Well, I'm certainly glad you're not sick of me, as I could see how it could happen—"

"Oh, stop." I smacked his arm playfully, and he pulled me closer.

"I'm just kidding. I think this time away has actually been good for us."

His arm was partway around my shoulder, and I placed a light kiss on the solid bicep that bulged through his long-sleeved shirt.

I nodded in agreement. "I actually think it has too. And I wasn't really mad at you. All this snow just has me feeling a little stir crazy. And seeing Erin here, and then watching her leave... Just knowing *she's* free to go anywhere."

"I know, I know." Adam drew me close and held me tightly. "We'll take some walks or something as soon as these storms pass. Just to get away from these four walls."

That sounded like heaven to me, and I told Adam as much. We sat awhile longer, just gathering comfort from relaxing in one another's arms.

At one point, Adam wound a lock of my hair around his fingers and asked, "Do you think about the future, Maddy?" Clearing his throat, he added, "Like *our* future, down the road?"

I thought about my future with Adam—a lot—and there was no doubt in my mind that I wanted to spend the rest of my life with him. We'd spoken words of *forever* during the past few months—and it was kind of assumed we were in this for the long haul—but we'd never specifically discussed where our relationship was heading.

"I think about our future often," I admitted. "And I want to be with you, Adam, only you, always. I love you."

"Do you think about children?" he asked, his tone hesitant, like he was feeling the idea out, seeing where my thoughts were on the subject.

I drew in a sharp breath but for the best possible reason. There was no other man whose children I'd rather bear. Adam Ward was it for me, so I meant it completely when I whispered, "Yes. And I'd want those children to be yours."

Adam straightened and turned to me so that we were facing one another. He held my gaze, his blue eyes...happy.

"I want all those things, too, Maddy. With you." He took a deep breath. "Marriage...children...a future... I want to grow old with you."

Tears welled in my eyes. I wanted those same things, so very, very much.

Adam said, "If we get through this—"

I quickly placed a finger across his soft, full lips, halting his words. "Not if, Adam, never if. *When* we get through this." He smiled and kissed my finger, still on his lips, and then he lowered my hand to his side.

"*When*," he said, stressing the word as I'd just done. "When we get through this, I want forever for us. But I want to do it right."

My heart filled with joy, as it sounded as if he planned to do what I'd only dreamed would someday happen. Adam Ward was going to ask me to marry him.

*

The next few days were perfect. The winter storms subsided, and Adam and I—as he'd promised—took long walks in the melting snow. It was only late February, but a hint of spring could be felt in the air. Spring. And for me and Adam—a deeper love.

On one of our strolls through the surrounding wilderness, trudging hand in hand through the heavy snow, Adam halted abruptly. Before I could ask what was wrong, he tucked me under his arm and pulled me close to his body.

I started to speak, but Adam shushed me. "Quiet, Maddy," he hissed.

When I glanced up, he nodded to a copse of pines several yards away. "Oh," I breathed out.

Now I got it.

Standing beyond the pines was a moose. Growing up in Maine, I was well aware the large animals were around, but I'd never seen one this close in the wild. The animal was magnificent, but I knew they could be dangerous. I snuggled in closer to Adam and whispered, "Will we be all right? What should we do?"

There was really nowhere to go. We were in the middle of the woods.

"We just have to wait him out," Adam whispered. "I don't think he's too concerned with us, as long as we stay back."

That sounded like a plan to me. My heart beat wildly. I sensed Adam was nervous too. His grip on me was iron-clad, his muscles tense.

We waited the animal out, and the moose eventually moved on.

Adam and I breathed out collective sighs of relief. We'd come out unscathed.

"He really was beautiful," I said to Adam once we were sure we were in the clear.

Adam agreed, but added, "I think we should return to the cabin."

I was fine with that.

The rest of the week rolled on, and another Friday arrived, which meant another visit from Agent Lenehan.

Oh, yay, I thought sarcastically.

It wasn't that I was still jealous of Erin—not like after I'd first met her. And I fully trusted Adam, even after my initial reactions to the agent's overwhelming beauty. My issue now was that I just liked the days…and nights…with Adam all to myself.

But since I was working on overcoming my insecurities—coupled with the fact Erin had been (mostly) nothing but nice to me since we'd met—I decided to make an overture of friendship to the woman who was essentially Adam's work partner. So, that Friday, I made enough food so Erin could stay for dinner.

While I worked on my signature eggplant parmesan, Adam prepared to go outside and chop some firewood.

"Mmm," Adam murmured as he passed through the kitchen on his way to the back door, "smells good, already." He paused at the stove and helped himself to a spoonful of simmering tomato sauce.

One spoonful turned to two, then three...

"Hey!" I playfully swatted his firm ass. "Stop eating all the sauce."

"I can't help it. It's really good, Maddy," Adam stated with a shrug, defending his actions.

Speaking of good, Adam looked mighty delicious himself. I stared at him, soaking in his fine profile, as he busied himself at the stove. He was now stirring the sauce instead of devouring it. He looked so sexy in his dark jeans and unzipped parka, his raven hair all messy and damp from a recent shower.

I suddenly wanted Adam, right there. Unfortunately, I knew our time alone was limited. Erin would be arriving soon.

Still, we had a few minutes. So, with no warning, I dropped to my knees in front of him and swiftly popped open the top button on his jeans.

"Maddy...what are you doing?" He set the spoon he'd been stirring with down with a clang.

"I think it's pretty obvious," I stated as I glanced up at Adam.

I hurriedly unzipped and lowered his jeans to just below his hips. Adam, of course, offered no resistance. He watched me in silence but let out a groan when I rubbed his rapidly hardening arousal through his boxer briefs. Soon, the gorgeous Mr. Ward was helping, particularly when I tugged his boxer briefs down. When his cock sprung free, I wasted no time. I took Adam in my mouth immediately, making him catch his breath.

I slid my lips along his shaft until his engorged head hit the back of my throat. "F-u-c-k," he rasped.

I took my time with him, cupping his balls, licking up and down his length, and swirling my tongue around the head of his penis. Despite being engaged as I was, I heard the echo of a car door closing outside.

Erin was here. But the thought of her being so close while I sucked off my boyfriend made the whole situation so much more arousing. Fortunately, it seemed Adam felt the same way. His breathing picked up as his pace increased. He wrapped his fingers in my hair, encouraging me to keep up with his rapid plunges into my mouth. Happy to oblige, I did exactly as he wanted. And when Agent Lenehan knocked on the back door, Adam came...hard.

"Hold on," Adam yelled over his shoulder as he caught his breath.

I stood up, and Adam tucked himself in and zipped back up. "Maddy, good thing all the windows are blacked out. You are bad, babe, very bad."

He smirked, letting me know that what he was really saying was that *bad, very bad* was actually good, very good.

"I'll have to be 'bad, very bad' more often," I chimed back, bumping his leg with my hip.

"Most definitely," he replied.

Adam stepped over to the door to let Erin in while I ran upstairs to brush my teeth and straighten my hair. When I returned to the kitchen, I got right back to work on finishing dinner. Adam and Erin had retired to the great room to talk Wickingham Way business. I peeked in at one point, and saw there were papers strewn all across the coffee table.

Erin was pointing out various things, and Adam was seated on the sofa, leaning forward and nodding thoughtfully.

I wondered what they were talking about. And at dinner I found out. Well, surely not everything but enough.

As we sat around the table in the kitchen, eating eggplant parmesan and drinking red wine, Erin continued with her updates to Adam, detailing the new developments in the Wickingham Way project.

I gathered that, thanks to Adam's most recent work, the criminal organization employing Stowe Hannigan was close to collapse.

"Financially crippled beyond repair," Erin said, confirming my assumptions. "The top-level associates have begun to scatter."

She explained that the government had already picked up many low – and middle-level members, some in Maine but mostly down in Florida. Many of the apprehended men were proving to be very helpful, as they were only too happy to exchange their testimony against some of the higher-ranking members for their own reduced charges.

The whereabouts of the very highest-ranking members, though, remained unknown.

The head of the organization, Nikolai's son, a man named Ruslan, was the one the government wanted the most. It was said he was cunning and ruthless, and he intended to rebuild his ruined empire. To capture him would mean the end of his organization...for good.

Unfortunately, no one could pinpoint Ruslan's exact whereabouts. This was especially disturbing to hear when it became pretty clear Ruslan was the one who'd issued the hit on Adam.

"So," I began as I set my fork down, "with Ruslan running around, Adam is still in danger, right?"

"Yes," Erin stated as she turned to me. "I'm afraid so, Maddy."

I then asked what I already knew, "Ruslan issued the directive to"—I swallowed hard—"kill Adam, right?"

Erin sighed. "Yes, Maddy, that's correct."

A few beats passed, allowing me several seconds to process this information.

Adam then asked Erin about the man who was probably the second-highest-ranking member of the organization that sought to off him. "What about Stowe Hannigan? Any word on him?"

Erin quickly lowered her eyes and stared down at her plate. She appeared to be studying what was left of her eggplant parmesan, but I swear the woman was blushing. Her cheeks were definitely turning crimson.

"Uh-h-h," Agent Lenehan drew out in an uncharacteristic shaky voice. "We're still working on Stowe Hannigan."

What kind of a response was that? Working on him? What did that mean?

I turned to Adam, but he just shrugged his shoulders and took a sip of wine.

Agent Lenehan's response was odd, to put it mildly. I suspected a story lay beneath her evasiveness.

Hmm…

Adam must have seen the wheels turning in my mind as he caught my attention and shook his head, as if to say, "Let it go."

I wished I were back in Harbour Falls. Then I could look into things. What was Agent Lenehan up to anyway? Why was she blushing at the mention of Stowe? Surely my charming, good-looking neighbor hadn't somehow won over one of the pivotal players in the Wickingham Way project, had he?

Good God, what if he had? Stowe Hannigan was a very persuasive, very handsome man. Hell, he'd charmed me…to an extent. But his intentions towards me had been harmless compared to this situation. If Agent Lenehan were compromised, I couldn't begin to imagine what that would mean for Adam…or for me.

I glanced around, suddenly feeling far less secure than I had before Erin's visit. I kept silent, but what I was really thinking was, *Just how safe is this safe house?*

Chapter Four

Despite my concerns, I knew the cabin would be safe for now. And that's all that really mattered. If trouble arose, then Adam and I would face it. But until that time, we were having far too much fun to worry.

Partially into the third week of our stay at the safe house, Adam and I took a break from all the reading we'd been doing. We shelved the books—for the time being—and dug out the board games Adam had told me about when we'd first come to the safe house. They were packed away in a crawl space on the second floor of the cabin.

Adam, feeling brave, volunteered to venture in and retrieve a few. When he emerged, he was carrying an armload of games. And he was covered in cobwebs.

"Aw, Adam, you look cute all dusty like this," I proclaimed as I brushed gray-white cobwebs from his raven hair.

Adam brushed a hand through his hair and rolled his eyes. "The things I do to keep you entertained," he playfully retorted.

Adam set the pile of games down, and I grabbed one from the top. "Oh, Monopoly," I cooed as I twisted the box in my hands and read the title. "Let's play this one first."

And so it was decided—Monopoly was up first.

I felt so certain I'd win that I bragged to Adam, "I used to always kick my brother's ass in this game." I blew on the dice and rolled. "So get ready to go down."

Adam laughed, smug. "We shall see about that, Maddy. You've never played this game with me."

No I had not. And an hour later, I came to the conclusion that Adam Ward was quite a different opponent than my brother, Brent, had ever been. Needless to say, I lost our first round of Monopoly. Badly.

"Damn Boardwalk!" I lamented when I ran out of money and all my properties were mortgaged.

I'd landed on the stupid square with the dark blue heading almost every time my poor little dog had made his way around the board, limping by the end. I accepted defeat gracefully, though, and promptly proposed a rematch.

To my chagrin, I lost that game as well.

"No more Monopoly," I groaned following my second crushing defeat.

Following a quick break for lunch, Adam held up some war-strategy game with the ominous title Risk.

Let's just say it was a bad move on my part to agree to play a game like Risk with the formidable Mr. Ward. I soon discovered Adam excelled at games where you either had to strategize or just flat-out take over the world. Adam was even better at that game than he had been at Monopoly.

"I give up," I said when I lost stupid Risk too.

In need of something a little simpler, I suggested Twister.

Adam laughed and said, "That's a kid's game, Maddy."

"Not really," I shot back. "After all, it was with the rest of the games you pulled out of the crawl space, right?"

"Only because when I brought those games from my parents' house—which was a long time ago, mind you—I just grabbed every game in sight."

I arched an eyebrow and smiled slyly.

"What?" Adam wanted to know.

"I think I know a way we can make Twister, um, more *adult*," I offered.

"And that would be…"

"Let's play naked Twister."

Yep, Adam *loved* that idea.

Entertaining from the start, the game turned especially so when Adam and I wound up all tangled up in each other. We eventually called the match a draw, but really I was the victorious one.

As I reminisced about everything Adam had done to me—with his knee on red and his hand on blue—the sound of his voice drew me from my lust-laced memory. I glanced up from where I sat perched, knees up, on the sofa. Adam was halfway down the stairs, holding up another game he'd pried from the pile.

"What do you think about this one, Maddy?" he asked, a playful grin in place on his beautiful face.

As I read the title, I laughed. "Clue?"

Adam glanced at the game, then back to me. "Well, yeah. I think this is a game you may actually have a possibility of winning," he deadpanned.

"Ha, ha, ha," I retorted.

Funny guy, that Adam Ward.

Of course, he had a point. I hadn't won a single game yet—if you didn't count our adult game of Twister. But if there was one thing I was good at, it was piecing together clues to get to the bottom of a mystery. History had proven that fact to be true. Hell, the more I thought about it, the more certain I became that this game was made for me.

"You're on, Ward," I declared resolutely as I stood. I straightened the fuzzy peach angora off-the-shoulder sweater I was wearing over my black camisole and brushed off my jeans. "Let's do it."

"Great," Adam said.

"Prepare for defeat," I added, pointing at the guy whose butt I planned to whoop as he came down the stairs.

Adam chuckled and strode toward me, game in hand. "Yeah, good luck with that," he muttered under his breath. "You're going to need it."

"Trash talker," I accused when he reached me.

"Just don't think I'm going to go easy on you, Fitch," Adam warned.

Damn, too bad he was talking about the game. Distracted momentarily, I took in how Adam's dark rinse jeans hugged his sculpted ass and how the dark gray sweater he was wearing showcased his finely toned upper body. Yeah. Adam was sex on legs, no doubt about it.

I smiled, and Mr. Sex-on-Legs promptly leaned down and gave me a quick peck on the cheek. He followed up with a playful smack to my ass right before we knelt down to spread the game board out on the floor.

"Trying to distract me?" I accused.

"Hey, whatever it takes."

"I am so going to kick your ass," I retorted.

Adam scoffed, but twenty minutes later my Miss Scarlet was indeed kicking Adam's Professor Plum's ass.

Yes! Perhaps I *could* win this one.

I carefully reviewed what I knew…

Okay, I was pretty certain the murder weapon was *the knife*, and the room the murder had been committed in was *the billiards room*. The only hitch—I was sketchy on the suspect.

Adam rolled the dice and moved his purple playing piece to *the library*. He cleared his throat and offered up his accusation. "I think it was Mrs. Peacock, in the library, with the knife."

Damn, Adam was onto *the knife* as the murder weapon, same as I suspected. With what I hoped was a poker face, I sorted through my cards. I held up the one for *the library*.

"Interesting," Adam murmured as he thumbed through his own cards.

I rolled the dice and worked my way toward the billiards room.

Once my token was in that green room, I took a stab (no pun intended).

"I think it was Mrs. White"—a pure guess—"in the billiards room, with the knife."

Adam's blue eyes met mine after he looked through his cards. "Huh. I think you may have won, Maddy."

"No way."

Adam examined his cards once more. "Yeah, you won. I don't have any of those cards."

I checked the cards we'd placed at the center of the board at the start of the game. I read the results out loud as I drew each one from the envelope: "Billiards room...knife... Mrs. White."

A beat passed, and then I tossed the cards in the air. "Oh my God, I won! I beat you, Adam."

Adam shook his head, but was smiling the whole time. He leaned across the board, cupped my chin, and kissed the tip of my nose. "Good game," he murmured as his thumb brushed over my lower lip.

"Do you want to play again?" I asked.

It was midafternoon, and there was a light snow falling. The temperatures were dropping, so it appeared we'd be staying indoors the remainder of the day.

Adam nodded. "Sure"—he glanced to the waning fire in the fireplace—"but let me grab more wood from outside before the snow picks up."

"Sounds good, I'll reset the game."

I began placing the different-colored playing pieces on their respective starting spaces, while, as per the usual routine, Adam worked to secure his .45 into the back of his jeans. Once that task was done, he opened the front door.

A cold wind blew in.

I watched Adam walk out to the porch, firearm visible, and sighed. Some days it was easy to forget why we were at this safe house, but the gun Adam kept nearby at all times served to harshly remind me he was in danger, always. We both were.

Just as I started to shuffle the cards, I heard the approach of a car, tires crunching through the snow and thick ice. Someone was pulling up to the house.

"What the…" I murmured to myself.

It was a Thursday, and Erin wasn't due to visit until Friday afternoon. So who was pulling up to the cabin?

I stood up and hurried to the door, concerned for Adam. And the exact second I was reaching for the doorknob, a single shot pierced the silence.

What the hell!

Panicked, I swung the front door open and took a single step out onto the porch. And that's where I froze as I took in the scene before me.

Adam was on the porch, in a shooter's stance, gun at the ready, while Erin crouched behind her car, taking cover from Adam's warning shot. The agent's voice rang out in the wintry stillness of the landscape, but I couldn't discern what the hell she was saying.

I gawked at Adam. "God, Adam, what are you doing?"

Had he lost his mind?

Adam threw me a quick sidelong glance, frowning. "Maddy, get back inside," he hissed.

Erin meanwhile, from behind her car, was shouting for Adam to put the gun down and listen. I couldn't imagine a single good reason why Adam would fire at Agent Lenehan, his trusted Boston contact. But then I saw movement next to her and realized she wasn't alone.

I squinted, and holy shit, I recognized the person who was with her.

Now I knew why Adam was firing. He wasn't shooting at Erin. Adam was shooting at the person with her—Stowe Hannigan.

Yeah, there was no mistaking the dirty-blond hair, very wide shoulders, and boyishly handsome face of the man who was hiding just under the line of the hood of the car. The man crouching next to Agent Lenehan was definitely Stowe Hannigan.

But what in the hell was Stowe doing *here* at the safe house? And why was he with *Erin*? More interestingly, why wasn't he shooting back?

Not that I wanted him to—dear God, no—but his job, after all, was to assassinate Adam.

Or was it?

I wasn't sure anymore, as Stowe sure wasn't making any moves to see the directive to kill Adam Ward to completion.

Adam walked slowly backward, nearing the door but never wavering with the gun.

When he was next to me, he said once again, "Get in the house, Madeleine."

His voice was low and even, but I knew he was steaming mad.

Before I could comply—or not—Erin yelled, "Adam, listen, Stowe is working with us. He has been for a while...I just couldn't say anything."

Well, that explained Erin's odd behavior every time Stowe's name had been mentioned.

"Please, Adam, put the gun down," she continued. "You know I wouldn't have brought Stowe here if he was a danger to you."

Adam kind of chuckled, like he didn't quite believe what she was saying. But I knew he ultimately trusted Agent Lenehan, so it wasn't a complete shock when, at last, he slowly lowered his weapon.

"This had better be good, Erin," Adam shouted out as the snow falling from the sky increased in intensity.

Agent Lenehan and Stowe stood cautiously from their safe positions behind the sedan. When it was clear Adam wasn't planning to shoot either one of them, they cautiously walked toward the porch.

Erin—dressed in black over-the-knee leather boots, designer jeans, and a smart gray overcoat—appeared more runway model than government agent as she swept her strawberry-blonde tresses over one shoulder and carefully made her way across the snow-covered land.

Stowe, in jeans and a dark parka, held Agent Lenehan's elbow in an effort to help her navigate the uneven drifts of snow in her high heels. I had to concede the two of them looked great together.

And that made me wonder if Stowe and Erin were a couple.

I was so busy focusing on Adam's contact and my former neighbor, and the possibilities, that I missed the look of fury on Adam's face. At least I did until the last minute. And it was in that moment, when Stowe and Erin stepped up to the porch, that Adam took a swing at the man he thought had tried to kill him.

"Adam, stop," both Erin and I cried out as Adam's fist met Stowe's jaw.

Stowe's head jerked to his right.

"That's for taking a shot at me on Fade Island," Adam said gruffly.

Stowe rubbed his jaw and replied, "Guess you wouldn't believe me if I told you it wasn't me on the island that day."

"Yeah, right," Adam scoffed, clearly not buying Stowe's claim of innocence.

Erin was quick to echo Stowe's words, though, coming to his defense.

Very interesting, I thought as Erin claimed the man who'd shot up Adam's study was someone else.

"Who?" Adam demanded.

"One of Ruslan's men," Erin stated. "He was apprehended leaving Maine the other day. He not only fits the description Max gave us, but we just recently procured his full confession."

Adam still didn't look fully convinced, but he grudgingly conceded it may not have been Stowe on the island that day.

"It was *not* Stowe," Erin insisted once more.

Erin sure was adamant, and it convinced me further that there was something going on with her and Stowe. Did Agent Lenehan have a thing for Stowe Hannigan?

It seemed so, I concluded when Erin reached up, touched Stowe's jaw gently, and said softly, "You should put some ice on that soon."

When Stowe saw as realization dawned on my face—and apparently Adam's too, as he smirked knowingly—he lowered Erin's hand back down to her side.

"I'm fine, Agent Lenehan," he replied curtly, his green eyes moving from me to Adam.

Stowe was trying to deflect by acting all professional with Erin. But it was too late. It was more than apparent there was something going on between them.

"Agent Lenehan," Adam *tsked* as he turned to Erin. "I'm surprised at you."

Erin blushed and whispered in a nowhere-near-convincing tone, "It's not what it looks like, Adam."

"Uh-huh," Adam replied skeptically.

I was still by the door and suggested we take the conversation inside, as the snow and winds were picking up.

"Hey," Adam barked as he placed a hand on Stowe's shoulder, halting his step across the threshold. The large man bristled, but Adam was undeterred. "You make one wrong move, you'll be sorry."

Stowe glanced down at Adam's now-secured firearm. "You think you're fast enough?" he taunted.

Adam scoffed, "I don't need a gun to stop you."

Stowe rolled back his broad shoulders, and Adam stood up straighter.

The two men, both powerful in their own right, sized each other up. I wondered who would win in a fight. Stowe was slightly taller and bulkier, but I knew Adam's lean build gave him an edge in quickness. No doubt it'd be a hard-fought battle, one I didn't care to witness any time soon.

Thankfully, Erin broke the tension when she gave the two men a withering look and stated, "Look, guys, it is fucking freezing out here. Let's move this dick-measuring contest indoors, all right?"

I giggled a little at her irreverence. I was beginning to like Erin a little more. Her comment got the guys moving too. Stowe stepped into the cabin, and Adam followed, keeping his stormy eyes on his nemesis's back.

Once we were all settled inside, I offered to make coffee. Adam, though, demanded I stay while he was told how it had come to pass that Stowe was now on the government's payroll.

"It's a long story." Erin sighed. "One we've been working on since way before the hit went out on you, Adam."

"You never mentioned anything," he retorted. "Shouldn't I have been apprised of these developments before today?"

"I couldn't say anything," Erin insisted. "I hadn't yet received clearance. When I was told it was okay to let you in on Stowe's involvement, it wasn't like I could pick up the phone and call you out here." She sighed. "Adam, I apologize for everything. I've wanted to say something for a long time now. I just...couldn't."

There were a lot more details, ones I figured weren't for my ears, so I excused myself to the kitchen to start brewing the coffee. When I returned to the great room, a tray of four steaming cups in hand, everyone seemed more relaxed with each other. However, I sensed there was another problem at hand. Worry hung in the room, making the air feel heavy. I just knew something bad had happened back in Harbour Falls.

Adam sat on a chair, positioned diagonally to the sofa, where Erin and Stowe were seated close together.

As I approached, Erin glanced at Adam. "We may as well tell Maddy," she said, her tone sad. "She's going to find out soon enough."

With a shaky hand, I set the tray on the coffee table. Stowe reached for a cup, but Adam and Erin remained still.

"Tell me what?" I queried, worried as to what could have possibly happened to have everyone looking so dour.

My eyes met Adam's, his blues filled with pity. *Huh?*

Adam looked away, and Erin stared at Stowe's cup on the table.

"Well…" I held out my hands beseechingly. "Is anyone going to say anything? What's going on?"

"You should probably sit down, Maddy," Stowe said.

Adam shot him a disdainful look, then stood and put his arm around my shoulder. He guided me to the chair he'd been sitting on.

My heart began to race. What was the problem here?

I slumped down to the chair, and Adam knelt down beside me. He held my hand and said, "Maddy, it's your dad—"

"What? What?" I started to stand, but Adam nudged me back into place.

I grasped and held his arm. "Adam, please, if something has happened to my father, I *have* to go back now."

A million scenarios ran through my head: heart attack, stroke, accident. But I never would have guessed this one:

"Maddy," Adam said, "your father has been kidnapped."

Chapter Five

My whole world spun. I was glad Adam had urged me to sit back down.

"No, no, no," I kept muttering.

"We'll get him back," I heard Adam say. "We have to return to Harbour Falls as soon as possible, though."

"But…we can't," I mumbled. "I mean, *you* can't."

My mind was a mess. I knew there was some reason why we couldn't go back, Adam in particular. But what was the reason again?

Oh, that's right; the hit was still out on Adam. And I, consequently, was in danger too.

But I couldn't lose my dad. Somewhere along the line, a sacrifice would have to be made. I waited for my eyes to fill with tears, but nothing happened. I felt too numb to cry.

It was then I realized I was slumped in the chair, still in the great room in the cabin, and Adam was still kneeling next to me, trying to get me to take a drink of water.

Oh, jeez. Had I passed out? For how long?

Stowe was leaning forward on the sofa, and Erin was crouched down next to Adam.

Agent Lenehan touched my forehead with a cool washcloth. "Everything will be all right, Maddy," she said.

I held the washcloth to my head. Erin let go, and I sat up straighter. I took a sip of the water Adam pressed to my lips.

Once I regained my composure, I sat up straight and demanded, "Who took my father? The organization you've been dismantling?"

Adam nodded grimly as he set the glass of water on the floor.

"How did this happen, Adam? Why would they take my dad?"

Erin and Adam exchanged a meaningful glance.

Adam exhaled loudly, then said, "Maddy, your father was a soft target, easy to reach. They made a grab for Nate, but he was too hard for them to get to."

"Nate's under protection like you?" I asked, even though I suspected that was the case.

"Yes," Adam confirmed, "as is Helena."

So, Nate was as involved as Adam in the Wickingham Way project. Not really a surprise there. And Helena being afforded protection was due to her being married to Nate. But my father, who I had worried for since the start of this trouble, had been left to fend for himself. And he'd never even been made aware he was in any trouble.

"Why wasn't my father protected?" I snapped.

Adam replied, "I'm sorry, Maddy. We had no idea anything like this would ever happen. Not to someone not directly involved with the Wickingham Way project."

"But Helena and I are under protection," I argued. "We're not directly involved. Why would my father be left unprotected?"

Adam sighed. "Decisions were made early on, calculated decisions. We expected Ruslan's organization to target spouses, girlfriends...but never *their* loved ones. You have to understand, Maddy, the only real threat left out there is Ruslan himself."

"And a few of his leftover henchmen," Erin chimed in.

Adam and I glanced at Stowe, and he put up his hands. "Not me. I've been out of it for a while now."

"So, why was my father taken?"

Stowe replied, "Because Ruslan is desperate, Maddy. He's grasping at straws."

Suddenly, all my anger, all my frustration, was redirected to the man who'd up until very recently been a part of this damn organization.

"You," I ground out, eyeing Stowe Hannigan. "This is all your fault, every last bit of it. You—you—you...bastard."

I couldn't help myself; my nerves were frazzled. So I launched myself at the one person who maybe could have stopped my father from being taken. Landing squarely on my former neighbor, my small fists began to make contact with his solid form. I hit and hit, pummeling away, until Adam dragged me off of Stowe.

"Shh, shh, Maddy, calm down," Adam whispered soothingly into my ear while wrapping me up in his arms.

He held me in place as I struggled to escape. "Let me go," I panted, ready to attack whoever was near.

When I finally calmed down, I glanced at Stowe. He appeared contrite but completely unharmed from all my punches. The only injury was the one to his jaw—still swollen from the punch Adam had thrown earlier out on the porch. And in that moment, I recognized that I wasn't really angry at Stowe. He was just bearing the brunt of my frustration.

"I'm sorry," I mumbled as I cast my eyes downward.

"No need to apologize," Stowe said. "I'm sorry I couldn't do more to stop your father from being taken. But

I promise from this point on that I'll do whatever it takes to rescue him."

I nodded and relaxed into Adam.

Adam sat down on the chair and positioned me on his lap. I curled up in his arms while he, Stowe, and Erin discussed where Ruslan and his minions may have taken my father.

"I think Ruslan is probably holding Mayor Fitch somewhere in Harbour Falls," Stowe stated, "or somewhere very close by."

Erin agreed and added, "Unfortunately, Maddy's dad was taken from his home, not from his office at city hall, so there's no video of his capture."

"That would have been very helpful," Adam chimed in.

"Definitely. Then, we'd know what"—Erin glanced at me, then quickly away—"condition to expect him in."

Adam cleared his throat. "It's very unlikely Mayor Fitch was harmed in any way."

Adam was saying that for my benefit, I knew it. However, I felt far from confident that my father, if unharmed upon capture, would remain so. I knew this organization had been deadly in its prime. And now the members remaining—ones on the run—were angry. The Wickingham Way project had left their organization in tatters, and they wanted Adam dead because of it. It hurt me to know I would have been the preferred target to lure Adam out of hiding. But I was here at the safe house with Adam. Because of my inaccessibility these evil people had gone after my father after trying, and failing, to capture Nate.

The conversation turned to strategies to employ when we returned to Harbour Falls, which, if all went well, would be by late tomorrow afternoon. Sadly, I didn't have a thing to contribute.

What could I do except get in the way?

I half-listened to everything Adam, Stowe, and Erin discussed, wishing I had something to add. But what it really came down to was that I just wanted my dad back. I didn't care how they did it, and I didn't need to be an integral part. I'd just do whatever was asked of me.

To my dismay, though, the only thing being asked of me at the moment was to make dinner.

"Everyone's getting hungry," Adam whispered to me. "Would you mind throwing something together?"

"Of course not," I replied. And then I went into the kitchen to get started.

When dinner was ready, everyone assembled around the table. But we ate in relative silence. I supposed we were all worn out. Erin and Stowe appeared especially tired, but even Adam seemed weary. Me, I was exhausted, though more mentally than physically.

After dinner, everyone pitched in to clean things up. And then we made our way upstairs to retire for the night.

Adam and I led Stowe and Erin to two separate bedrooms down the hall from where Adam and I slept. Erin turned to Adam as we neared the end of the hall and told him she and Stowe needed only one bedroom.

Adam's eyebrow rose. "Not what it looks like, eh?" he scoffed, making reference to her earlier comment regarding her relationship—or lack thereof—with Stowe.

Okay, so the two of them had something going on. They were obviously sleeping together.

Adam mumbled something off-color about them sleeping in the same room, and Erin smacked his arm and shot back, "Shut up, Adam."

To my surprise, despite her comment, Erin didn't seem angry at all. Adam chuckled, and Erin smiled.

I once would have been jealous of the easy camaraderie Erin and Adam were displaying. But now I valued it. The fact that Adam and Erin worked so well together—and got along like brother and sister—boded well for finding my father. I was relying on their good partnership. And having Stowe on board could only help...I hoped.

Once Adam and I were in our own bedroom, I asked him what he thought about Stowe switching sides. "Do you think he's legit?"

I tugged the sweater I was wearing over my head and discarded my jeans, leaving me in just a camisole and underwear. "Can he really be trusted?"

Adam stripped down to his boxer briefs. My gaze moved upward, and I watched as the muscles in his shoulders and arms flexed, especially as he pulled the bedding back from the bed.

"I do think his switching-sides is legit," Adam stated after a thoughtful pause. "I didn't at first...obviously"—a reference to his attempt this afternoon to shoot Stowe—"but I have to say I felt more sure after speaking with Erin privately. It's actually a smart move on Stowe's part—better to side with your enemy than be crushed by it."

Adam had a point, but..."Can he be trusted?"

Adam shrugged. "I don't know, Maddy. But Erin sure seems to think so."

"Is she a good judge of character?" I asked, truly curious.

"Time will tell."

"That's not very reassuring," I scoffed.

Adam sighed. "I'm not supposed to say anything, Maddy, but Erin told me in confidence that Stowe has been on board with the Wickingham Way project for a while now...a *long* while."

"How long?" I asked, curious since this bit of information could determine just how committed Stowe was to
helping us.

Adam held my gaze and replied, "Since December."

"December..." I echoed as we crawled into bed at the
same time, me on one side, Adam on the other.

Huh. No wonder Stowe had been so kind to me from the
first day I'd met him. He'd been looking out for me as far
back as January. All because I was with Adam, even though
neither Adam, nor I, knew Stowe's true identity—or intentions—back then.

I am not the bad guy, Stowe had said to me.

His switching sides must have been what he'd been
referring to all along. He knew I'd eventually find out he
was an assassin, and he knew word would get back to me
that there was a hit out on Adam. He also knew there might
never be a way to tell me he was on the good side of the
Wickingham Way project.

And that begged the question: Had Stowe purposely
left those files out on the table in his dining room? Is that
why he'd left his house that morning and stayed away for
such a long while? Stowe was quite familiar with my curiosity issues. He had to have surmised I'd go snooping around
after what had happened at Willow Point—after Stowe had
saved Helena and me from her psycho stepfather.

I'd thought at the time that Stowe was just completing a directive for the criminal organization we mistakenly
thought he was with at the time. But perhaps he'd truly
been protecting *me.*

Well, in any case, one thing was certain: Stowe on our
side was better than Stowe against us. After all, he *was* a
calculating killer. Switching to our side didn't change that

little fact. But the question remained: Would Stowe kill to save my father?

That I didn't know. But I did know my father didn't deserve to have been pulled into this mess. *I* should have been the one who'd been taken.

"Ruslan chose my dad to lure you out," I stated, turning to Adam, who was lying on his back.

I suspected as much but wanted confirmation.

"Yes." Adam shifted so he could face me.

The small lamp by the bed was on, and Adam's face was bathed in a warm golden glow. I reached over to trail my hand down his cheek. When I reached his jaw, there was the slightest hint of stubble. I cupped him there. "So, you have to put yourself back in danger in order to save my dad?"

The lump that had taken up residence in my throat made it difficult for my words to pass freely.

Seeing how upset I was becoming, Adam gathered me into his arms. "Maddy, Maddy," he said as I choked back a sob. "I will be fine. We'll get your father back, even if it means a trade."

"What?" I glanced up at Adam. "A trade? What trade? Adam, you can't do that." My voice went up an octave. "No way. They'll kill you."

Adam kissed my forehead. "Let's not think about it right now, okay? We'll know more once we're back in Harbour Falls. We'll assess the situation then."

I murmured a halfhearted, "Okay."

My father was a "situation"; Adam risking his life was a "situation." I wasn't sure how I felt about all that, but I did know I wanted to forget everything for just one night—tonight.

"Kiss me, Adam," I breathed out.

"Maddy..." His hand fisted in my hair as he pulled me closer.

Our lips met in a heated frenzy. Adam seemed as hyped up as I, but I sensed his urgency had more to do with his nemesis, Stowe Hannigan, sleeping down the hall.

If Stowe had been sleeping, though, he wasn't for long. Things grew noisier and noisier as Adam handled me roughly, hauling me up on all fours.

Foreplay was rushed, but it didn't matter; I was more than ready. Still, when Adam sheathed himself inside of me to the hilt with one stabbing thrust, I cried out. I felt a mixture of pleasure and pain, but I begged him not to stop. I needed to be taken like this in order to forget. Most of the sex we'd been having at the cabin had been rather tame, gentle, and loving.

Hell with that.

It'd been a while since Adam had behaved so aggressively, so forcefully. But he manhandled me now, his fingers digging into my hips as he held me in place and fucked me raw. His savagery brought me to orgasm again and again.

When Adam came, he flattened me to the mattress with his body. His teeth latched on to my neck as I felt him empty into me. I cried out, but the sound was muffled by the pillow.

Once Adam regained a steady breath, he shifted his weight off of me and made sure I was all right.

I rolled my eyes as he checked my body. "I'm fine, Adam." I sighed, feeling perfectly contented.

Adam's fingers lingered where he'd left a light bruise mark on my hip. "I'm sorry," he said, his lips kissing the mark tenderly.

I insisted again that I was fine, and I was. I'd wanted things rough, same as Adam.

"I've had worse bruises from bumping into furniture," I told him, my words true.

"Still," Adam muttered.

I changed the subject. "Wow, I bet we woke Erin and Stowe up with all the noise we made."

Adam chuckled, and with the way he was smirking I knew that had been his plan all along. "I bet you're right," he concurred, smug.

"Maybe they didn't notice," I threw out just to rankle Adam. "Who knows? They could have been doing the same thing."

"Not as good as us, baby," Adam said. "And regardless, I am quite sure they heard."

Adam was probably right. Erin and Stowe would have had to be comatose to miss *that*.

In a way, I kind of liked the thought that Erin, specifically, had heard. Just so there was no doubt in her mind that Adam belonged to me. I supposed that made me just as territorial as Adam, but I didn't really care. Two could play at that game.

Adam was right about the other thing he's said, as well. We *were* good together. But not just in regards to sex. Adam and I were good as a couple.

In many ways we were a perfect match. Which was why that night, as I nodded off to sleep, I felt a newfound confidence that my father would be rescued, and everything would turn out right.

I just didn't anticipate what it might eventually cost.

Chapter Six

The ride back to Harbour Falls was…interesting. The testosterone-fueled tension between Adam and Stowe was palpable in the confines of the car Erin drove. Agent Lenehan shifted uncomfortably in the driver's seat as a result.

I sighed. *Yeah, I feel it too, Erin. I feel it too.*

The fact remained that, despite the sort-of truce that had been reached at the cabin, Stowe and Adam just didn't get along very well. They hadn't for ages, and one twenty-four-hour period of peace wasn't about to change that. Animosity between the two strong-willed men had taken hold long ago, back when Adam dated—and was then engaged to—Stowe's sister, Chelsea.

Here in the car now, it was evident not much had changed over the years.

Stowe, seated in the passenger seat up front, stared straight ahead, jaw set and fists clenched at his sides. Adam, conversely, who was seated next to me in the backseat, alternated between fussing over me and shooting daggers to the back of Stowe's head.

The fussing I enjoyed. The dagger shooting to Stowe's head, I could have lived without.

Damn.

I was worried sick trying to figure out how these two stubborn men were ever going to work together peacefully. And I needed them to do exactly that, for my father's sake.

Throwing fuel on an already simmering fire, Adam, out of the blue, asked, "So, did everyone sleep all right last night?" His tone was nothing short of taunting, smug.

My face burned hot, while Erin stifled a cough. Stowe shifted uncomfortably. Clearly, the two front-seat occupants had heard Adam's lusty encounter with me last night.

If there was any doubt about it, though, that doubt was squashed when Stowe flippantly tossed out over his shoulder, "Kind of hard to sleep with all the noise. But we managed." He gave Erin a wink, and she smiled tightly.

Adam chuckled and apologized.

But he was so not sorry. Adam wanted Stowe to hear everything last night. That's why he'd been so aggressive. Not that I hadn't loved every minute of it. Oh, had I ever. Adam had claimed me last night, partly to ensure Stowe Hannigan kept in mind that I was completely off-limits. I belonged to one man only: Adam Ward.

Even though Stowe and Erin appeared to be some sort of a couple these days, there had been a time when my neighbor had expressed interest in me. Stowe had never acted on his attraction—and he remained my friend during the whole Willow Point ordeal—but I knew his presence in my life at the time had irked Adam. The powerful Mr. Ward did not like to be challenged, and Stowe presenting me with flowers, bringing wine to a dinner he and I shared alone, and just generally spending time with me were all viewed as definite challenges.

However, there'd never been any need for Adam to worry. I was clear with Stowe from the start. My heart belonged to Adam, then and now.

Erin's eyes met mine in the rearview mirror. She rolled her chocolate browns and mouthed, "Boys."

I giggled a little, and Adam shot me a questioning look. I just shrugged.

"So," I began, changing the subject, "what's the plan for when we're back in Harbour Falls?"

The more pressing matter was how we planned to rescue my father from the clutches of what remained of the criminal organization Adam had essentially crushed. Before leaving the safe house, we'd all agreed no law enforcement entities were to be called in, with the exception of the feds who were already involved in the Wickingham Way project. We'd also discussed how to handle the sure-to-arise questions regarding the missing mayor. We planned to issue a press release, stating that Mayor Fitch was vacationing in the Caribbean.

Oh how I wished that was actually the case.

My father was a good man; he had no business getting tangled up in this Wickingham Way web. But alas, here we were—heading back to Harbour Falls to save my dad.

We'd already enlisted two other people's help. Max had been notified of our impending return yesterday evening, and Nate was also up to speed. Both men would have roles in my father's rescue, though I had no clue what those roles would be.

However, I was about to find out.

Stowe mentioned something about going over the plan once again, and Erin's eyes met mine in the rearview mirror. "Maddy," she began, "once we're back in Harbour Falls, it is absolutely imperative you're seen. The few men still with Ruslan will get word back to their boss once you're spotted. Afterward, we expect Ruslan to make contact. He'll naturally assume, rightfully so, that Adam has returned with you."

Ruslan was still running what remained of the criminal organization the Wickingham Way project had crippled. He had been since the fall, when his father, Nikolai, had passed away. Odd, I thought, how one man's death had precipitated the entire Willow Point ordeal. And we were still dealing with the fallout all these months later.

Erin drew my attention back to her when she said, "Ruslan knows Stowe is with us, but he believes it's only to infiltrate our organization in order to get to Adam. Therefore, we're going to have Stowe set up the trade for your father."

"Who are we trading for my dad?" I cautiously ventured.

When I received no immediate answer, I knew the answer was Adam.

"No way." I turned in my seat to face my guilty-looking guy, who was staring straight ahead so as to avoid my questioning gaze.

"Hey," I continued, "I thought we decided last night we'd assess the situation once we're back in Harbor Falls? There has to be a way to save my dad without risking you. Right, Adam?"

When no one answered, my voice grew frantic. "Adam?" I tried to catch Agent Lenehan's eyes in the rearview mirror since Adam was essentially ignoring me. "Erin?"

Adam turned his head to stare out the side window, and Erin kept her focus on the road.

It was Stowe who finally piped up with, "We're not going to really trade Adam for your father, Maddy. It's just a setup to help us pinpoint where Ruslan is holding your dad. Once we know where he's holed up, we can go in and rescue your dad."

"Oh, okay," I mumbled.

I was still uneasy about the whole thing. I mean, why were Adam and Erin so reticent to speak? I certainly hoped Stowe was telling me the whole truth. But I had to wonder when Adam kept his eyes averted. I had a feeling I was not being given the entire story. And if that was the case, then why? What else was going on here? Did the government want Adam to get close enough to Ruslan to kill him? Good God, I hoped not. However, I had to admit, it was a distinct possibility.

So just how deeply was Adam involved in all of this?

The criminal organization Wickingham Way had been designed to bring down was essentially destroyed. So why was Adam still so involved with the ongoing operation?

When I flat-out asked that exact question, everyone remained silent.

"Is someone going to fill me in on why Adam is still involved?" I pressed.

Adam placed a comforting hand on my knee. "Maddy…" He blew out a breath. "My role in this operation isn't over until Ruslan is…incapacitated."

"You mean dead, right?"

Adam nodded, his expression somber.

My voice hitched as I asked in a shaky voice, "Are *you* going to be the one to kill him, Adam?"

I barely heard his response as he whispered, "Maybe, Maddy, maybe."

Now it was all clear.

Adam *was* going to trade himself for my father. This plan was about more than just pinpointing Ruslan's location and rescuing my dad. In exchanging himself for my father, Adam could possibly get close enough to Ruslan to kill him. And a dead Ruslan would ensure the criminal organization the government had been so set on destroying would *never* be rebuilt.

Jeez, these guys are hardcore.

"Well," I stated defiantly, "if you're really going to go to Ruslan, then I'm going with you."

I received three resounding *no way* responses.

Stowe added, "Adam won't be alone, Maddy. And whoever reaches Ruslan first will be the one to..."

Stowe let that sentence dangle, but I knew what he was saying—first person to reach Ruslan would take him out.

I'd seen Adam handle firearms with ease. At the lighthouse months ago, and just the day before, when Stowe showed up with Erin at the safe house. But just how well-trained was he? Was Adam an operative of some sort?

"Do you work for them?" I asked under my breath. "Like on a regular basis?"

Adam knew I was asking if he was some sort of an agent, like Erin.

He shook his head. "No, my business is in computer security, Madeleine. As you already know."

"Then why—"

Adam interrupted me. "This case is different, Maddy. It was my decision to agree to see it to its conclusion."

"Okay," I drawled, still a little confused.

And then it hit me; Adam was still a part of the Wickingham Way project for *me*, for my protection. Until Ruslan was neutralized—permanently—there'd forever be a price on Adam's head. And that meant I would remain in danger as well.

"Damn," I mumbled as the full implication of Adam's involvement washed over me like an icy cold wave.

I shuddered, and Adam pulled me close to him.

I realized there was no other way. My dad needed rescuing, and Ruslan had to be stopped for good. And if that meant Adam would have to become a killer, then I'd have to accept it.

Didn't mean I ever had to learn to like it.

Chapter Seven

When we arrived at my Victorian rental in Harbour Falls, Nate and Helena were waiting on the walkway leading to the porch.

I practically jumped out of Erin's car to run to and embrace Helena. She'd become my best friend in Harbour Falls, and I'd missed her quite a bit the past few weeks.

"Maddy," Helena squealed as I threw my arms around her. "I'm so glad you're back. I missed your visits to the café."

Helena and I had grown close since ever since my arrival back in town in the fall, but we'd really bonded after what happened up at Willow Point. After our ordeal, we'd visited one another almost daily until Adam and I had been forced to leave the area. But now we were back, ready to resume our lives. Well, after we rescued my dad and dispatched Ruslan, of course.

"I missed you, too," I said to Helena as I gave her one last squeeze, before stepping back.

Helena and I took the moment to assess one another, and then we simultaneously blurted out, "You look great."

Everyone laughed, and Adam and I took the opportunity to introduce our friends. Nate and Helena already knew Stowe, of course. Stowe just nodded a hello, then hung back to let us continue the introductions. Nate knew Erin from working with her on the Wickingham Way project, but Helena had yet to officially meet Agent Lenehan.

"Nice to meet you," Helena said as she shook Erin's hand.

I'd forgotten how pretty Helena Jackson was. She certainly held her own next to the stunning Erin. Helena was a gorgeous woman in her own right—long blonde tresses, soft features, pretty blue eyes. And Nate was just as attractive—mocha-toned skin, amiable brown eyes, making the two of them together a rather stunning couple.

I glanced over at Nate, and he gave me a smile. "It's good to have you and Adam back," he said quietly. "Just wish it was under different circumstances."

I nodded once and looked down at the walkway. Helena touched my arm. "Hey, your father is going to be okay, Maddy."

I pressed my lips together so I wouldn't start crying. I prayed Helena's words would prove prophetic.

Adam cleared his throat and suggested we go into the house, since it was rather cold to stand around outside.

Once we were all inside the Victorian, I excused myself to the kitchen to make coffee for everyone.

Helena followed, and I said to her over my shoulder, "Seems like all I do nowadays is make coffee for everyone."

Helena laughed. "Ha, try running a café. You'll get so sick of serving coffee that you'll want to scream."

"Good point," I replied as we stepped into the kitchen. Sighing, I added, "I missed this. It's good to be back, even if the circumstances are crummy."

"I know, Maddy. I'm happy you're back. I just wish..." She trailed off, which was just as well.

I didn't want to think about my father being held captive somewhere. If I did, with the way I felt right now, I'd lose it. I busied myself with reaching for four coffee cups that were up high on a shelf, but when I wasn't able to grasp the two in the back, Helena, who was much taller than me, retrieved them.

"Thank you," I said.

We sat down at the kitchen table and waited for the coffee to brew.

"So, how was the safe house?" Helena asked, one eyebrow rising suggestively.

I knew Helena well enough to know she wasn't asking about the décor. Nope, she wanted the down and dirty details of my time alone with Adam. She was not only trying to be a friend and keep my mind off my dad, but Helena flat-out loved to gossip. She especially adored girl talk, particularly the naughty variety.

I didn't mind sharing some details of my alone time with Adam. Some things—like chatting up your hot guy with your good friend—just never got old. With that thought in mind, I got right to it.

"Oh my God, Helena." I drummed a hand on the table and suppressed a silly-girl squeal. "I cannot begin to tell you how amazing it was having Adam all to myself out there in the woods." I sighed contemplatively. "No work interruptions, no business trips, no Fade Island concerns… It was heaven."

"Hmm," Helena hummed, "that good, huh?"

"Yep," I confirmed, "it was great."

"What about the sex?" she asked slyly.

I giggled. "Well, let's just say Adam is a sex god."

"I don't doubt it," Helena replied matter-of-factly. "Adam is a hottie."

"He is," I agreed.

Helena laughed, but then added in a serious tone, "Hey, don't tell him I said that about him. Adam already has a big enough ego."

"That's not the only thing that's big." I waggled my eyebrows.

"Ugh." Helena smacked my arm. "I do not need to hear that much detail. I think of Adam as a brother, and I'd like to not think about his big dick every time I see him."

I busted out laughing, and Helena soon joined me. I also solemnly promised not to give her any more detail on Adam's impressive, er, assets.

"Things must be great with you and Nate, too," I began, smoothly changing up the subject to her and her husband. "You both look really happy."

Helena smiled and nodded. "We are, Maddy. And I have to say, with all that terrible stuff regarding my stepfather behind us, it's like a weight has been lifted from our shoulders."

"I'm sure."

"Oh, by the way," Helena whispered as she glanced back to the doorway. "I have to tell you something, something important."

"What is it?" I asked worriedly, hoping she didn't have some kind of bad news.

Thankfully, her news was fantastic!

"I'm pregnant," Helena exclaimed.

"Oh my God." I was so excited for her that I leaned over and hugged her tightly. "Helena, this is so incredible. I'm so happy for you and Nate."

Truly, I was thrilled. Nate and Helena had been married for almost a decade, but had never been blessed with children.

"It finally happened, Maddy," Helena said into my hair. Her voice cracked as she held onto me.

I planned to ask Helena for some details, like how far along she was, but Erin unfortunately chose that exact moment to walk into the kitchen.

I leaned back in my chair while Helena wiped at her eyes.

"I'm sorry," Erin said when she realized she'd walked in on a private moment. She gestured to the doorway. "Uh, I can leave—"

"No, no," Helena interrupted with a wave of her hand. "Don't be silly. Come on in and join us."

Erin pulled out a chair and sat down hesitantly. The coffee was ready, so I got up and poured three cups.

"We'll take some in for the guys in a minute," I said as I passed out the coffees and sat back down.

Erin thanked me and lifted her cup to her lips. "I'm sorry Stowe acted the way he did in the car." She took a small sip of coffee and set the cup back down. "I mean with Adam."

"Oh..." I waved my hand dismissively. "It's no big deal. Adam and Stowe just don't get along. It goes way back, but they're obviously still ridiculously competitive with each other."

"Yeah, I noticed that last night," Erin mumbled into her cup as she took another sip.

I suppressed a laugh, well aware of what Erin was referring to.

Helena, though, was confused. She asked, "What? What happened last night?"

Helena glanced from Erin to me. Awaiting details, I supposed.

I felt my cheeks heat. I wasn't embarrassed to tell Helena about last night, but I was hesitant to discuss my love life with Erin. Of course, she'd already *heard* quite a lot, thanks to Adam and his damn competitiveness with Stowe Hannigan.

Helena said, "I'm waiting."

So…I spilled the beans.

"Uh, just, Adam was rather…exuberant last night in bed. I guess we got kind of loud."

Helena laughed and shook her head.

"Exuberant? Loud? That's putting it mildly." Agent Lenehan took another sip of coffee. "At one point, Stowe and I thought we might have to come in and rescue you."

I knew Erin was joking, so I thought, *What the hell?* We were having fun; I decided to just go with it.

"You sure would have gotten an eyeful if you'd done that," I muttered.

Erin replied, "I don't doubt it. Adam can certainly be intense. I mean, he's pretty intense when it comes to work. And from what I heard last night, he's obviously that way in *other* areas of his life as well."

Again, though I knew it was silly, a tiny pang of jealousy reverberated through me. It was clear Erin knew Adam well enough to have had opportunities to observe my man's intensity.

Oh well. I was just glad the agent who worked so closely with Adam was now with Stowe.

And that made me curious…

"So-o-o." I rested my chin on my hand and eyed Erin. It was her turn to give up the goods. "Now that we all know how competitive those two are, I'm guessing maybe Adam might have…I don't know…possibly *inspired* Stowe last night."

Helena shot me a wide-eyed, raised brow look that screamed, *I can't believe you just asked that.*

But I had, and now it was Erin's turn to blush.

The usually cool and collected agent played nervously with a strand of her strawberry blond hair. "Uh, actually..."

"Yes?" I wasn't letting this woman off the hook. She was obviously close with Adam, so she may as well get close to me too.

Or so I reasoned. But, truth be told, I was also insanely curious.

Erin took another sip of coffee, while Helena and I waited. Hell, Helena seemed to be just as curious as I was now that her initial surprise at my brazenness had subsided.

"Okay, okay." Erin set down her cup and smiled.

In satisfaction, it seemed to me. I imagined her reviewing in her mind what she and Stowe had ended up doing last night.

I tapped my cup in anticipation, and at last, Erin lowered her voice and said, "Actually, I think Stowe *was* inspired by Adam. I have to say, Maddy, he did things to me last night that I didn't think he had in him."

My mouth gaped. I was shocked. *Didn't think he had it in him?* Stowe was hot, he was dangerous, and he'd been a criminal up until just a couple of months ago. And Erin herself could be rather dangerous. So what could Stowe possibly have done that was so surprising to Miss Secret Agent?

I was dying to ask, insanely curious as always, but I didn't have the nerve to keep prying.

Helena did, though. "Ooh, so what'd he do?" she asked without hesitation. "Stowe is so big and buff and manly, so I can only imagine."

Erin hesitated, then took a breath. She opened her mouth but stopped.

I was sure we'd never find out, but finally she began, "Okay, so you both know Stowe and I carry handcuffs, right?"

Helena and I nodded in unison. There was a dishrag on the table, and Helena snatched it up and started twisting it in her hands. My friend was as rapt with attention as I.

"Well, I also have a set that can be secured around the ankles."

I was speechless, but Helena asked what I was secretly thinking. "Who handcuffed whom?"

"Stowe handcuffed me. Uh, face down on the bed," Erin whispered. "And then he—"

"Hey, babe," Nate said to Helena as he walked in and unknowingly interrupted Erin's salacious story. "Where's that coffee? We've been waiting forever."

"Damn it, Nate." Helena threw the dishrag at him.

He caught it easily. Nate apparently knew his wife quite well, for as he walked to the counter where the coffeepot sat, he said, "Aah, I'm interrupting some kind of little tawdry sex discussion, aren't I? No wonder you forgot to bring in the coffee."

Little tawdry sex discussion? Ha, if Nate only knew. We ladies could outtalk the men when it came to sex.

Helena's husband poured three cups of java—for himself, Stowe, and Adam—then left, smiling and shaking his head. But the moment for risqué storytelling had been lost.

Erin's expression grew serious. "We should join the guys in the living room. We have a lot to discuss."

She was right. We had yet to finalize the plan—the plan for rescuing my poor kidnapped father. The respite from the seriousness of the situation we faced was over.

Erin rose and refilled her coffee. I remained seated at the table, and Helena covered my hand with hers. "Are you all right?"

I nodded once. "I guess."

Erin left, saying she'd be in the living room, waiting with the guys.

I sighed and turned to Helena. "It was just nice to forget about what's going on for a little bit."

"I know, Maddy, I know."

Helena and I rose and refilled our cups and then headed to the living room.

Lighthearted girl-talk time was over. Sadly, we were back to dealing with harsh realities.

Chapter Eight

The excitement over Helena's pregnancy and the curiosity as to what kinds of kinky things Stowe was in to would have to wait...at least, for the time being.

Helena and I stepped into the living room and sat down at the end of the sofa, where Nate and Stowe made room for us. Adam and Erin, seated in chairs nearby, waited for us to get settled.

"Okay," I said after a minute. "How's this going down?"

Adam shuffled some papers and then began to review the plan that had been devised to rescue my father. The reality and the seriousness of the undertaking splashed over me like a bucket of ice water. My father was in real peril. He could even end up...dead. I guessed I'd been trying not to think about how my dad was being held captive by the remaining members of a ruthless organization, tattered though it was at the moment. But now I had no choice but to face facts—like how Adam was going to put himself in jeopardy to rescue my father. All because he loved me, which was why I piped up at one point and asked if there was possibly another way to save my dad.

I was told no. The plan was set, and everything was final.

It sure was final; the very next day the plan went into motion.

As Erin had mentioned on the car ride back to Harbour Falls, it was imperative that I was seen out and about in town. But not with Adam. That would be way too obvious, arousing suspicion that our return to Harbour Falls was a setup, which it was, of course, but Ruslan didn't need to know that little fact.

So when I headed over to my father's house—the stately white-frame structure in which I'd grown up—it was Erin who accompanied me. She was there as a friend but also as protection. I knew somewhere under the smart business pantsuit she was wearing there was a hidden firearm.

I felt safe with Erin, but still, she was only one person. Who knew how many men Ruslan had working for him in Harbour Falls?

"Shouldn't we have more cover?" I asked Erin as I made an unnecessary turn. I was trying to take the longest route possible to maximize opportunities for me to be seen.

"Look around, Maddy," Erin replied as she twisted in the passenger seat to face me. "We're not as alone as you might think."

"Really?"

I was doubtful until I really began to pay attention to the cars around us. I quickly realized we were being shadowed.

"The car behind us..." I nodded up to the rearview mirror to bring attention to the plain, dark sedan tailing us. "Is that an agent?"

"Yes, Maddy," Erin assured me. "He's one of many."

The extra agents made me feel more secure but also uneasy. It stood to reason that if our people were around—ones I hadn't even noticed, at first—then Ruslan surely had people tailing us as well.

But that's what we want, I reminded myself. The plan was for me to be seen. And then Stowe would wait for Ruslan to (hopefully) make contact.

I'd been informed Ruslan was still under the impression Stowe worked for him. He thought my neighbor was only on the Wickingham Way project as a mole of some sort. How wrong he was.

Anyway, continuing with what I'd been told of the plan...

After contact was initiated, Stowe would confirm to Ruslan that Adam was indeed back in Harbour Falls. And then a trade would be arranged—Adam for my father. Once a location was chosen—by Ruslan—Stowe and Adam would meet up with the crime boss to complete the trade. Unbeknownst to Ruslan, however, Nate would also be with them, and possibly Max.

The deal would never happen. If all went well, my father would be whisked away to someplace safe, and Ruslan would be terminated. I still held out hope that Stowe—or Nate—would be the one to kill the man. I really didn't want Adam to do it.

Throughout the years following Chelsea's disappearance, so many people had suspected Adam of playing a role in her untimely departure. Many believed he had murdered his fiancée to end her blackmailing scheme. But Adam did not kill Chelsea or anyone else. And I didn't want him to start killing people now, even the bad ones.

Damn, I'll be glad when all this is over, I thought. *Then Adam and I can get back to each other.*

During our time at the cabin, Adam had asked me where I planned to live, permanently. He wanted to know if I ever intended on going back to California...or if I had maybe considered staying on in Maine. I'd actually thought about it a lot, so I was able to give Adam an answer right away. I planned to remain right where I was—in Harbour Falls.

Adam had been elated, especially when I told him I'd already made arrangements with Katie, my best friend and agent, to put my Los Angeles house up for sale. Upon hearing that news, Adam promptly asked me to move in with him on Fade Island. Of course, I had agreed.

There was so much good ahead of us.

I smiled to myself as I counted off all the positive developments. One, I'd finished my novel—the love story inspired by my relationship with Adam—and sent it off to my publisher earlier that morning. And two, with Helena pregnant, I wanted to start planning a baby shower for her. She'd mentioned that the baby was due in early October, so I was thinking of throwing the shower in September. On top of all those positive developments, there were still preparations to be made for Trina and Walker's upcoming wedding, as well.

Adam's sister and her fiancé were getting married in May, down in Boston. Adam was to be Walker's best man, and to my surprise and delight, Trina had asked me to be a bridesmaid.

I must have still been smiling as we reached the driveway of my father's house. When I pulled in and placed the car in park, Erin asked me what I was thinking about that was making me so happy.

I told her about Adam's sister's upcoming nuptials.

"I just hope all of this will be over by then." I tapped at the steering wheel, worried. "The wedding is only six weeks away. I can't imagine Adam participating if he's still a target." I took a deep breath. "And God forbid if my dad isn't rescued by then."

Erin turned in her seat. "Your father will be rescued, Maddy. I promise. The backup team will be in place. If things aren't going well with the original plan, they'll swoop in."

If things aren't going well with the original plan... What did that mean exactly?

I was afraid to ask what constituted failure in the eyes of the ruthless, covert branch of government Erin worked for. I cared for all four men—Adam, Nate, Max, and Stowe—to varying degrees. And though Adam's safety was and always would be my top priority, I would never forgive myself if any of the four didn't make it out from the rescue attempt unscathed.

That included my father, of course.

I leaned back in my seat and ran my hands down my face. "So, what are we supposed to do here at my dad's house? Is it good enough if they see us in the driveway, or should we go in?"

"We should probably go in and stay for a few minutes." Erin appeared thoughtful for a beat, and then she asked, "Is there something you can carry out of the house as we're coming back out? It will make this stop appear more legitimate if Ruslan is told you really were here to pick something up."

I considered. "Hmm, I have some clothes from way back. They're up in my old room. I could put some things in a box and carry it out. Would that work?"

"That'd be perfect, Maddy." Erin lifted the handle and opened the passenger side door. "Let's get started."

As we walked into my childhood home, I asked, "How long should we stay?"

"Not too long. Fifteen, twenty minutes should be good."

To waste a little time, I showed Erin around the down-stairs area, grabbing up an empty cardboard box before we left the kitchen. I led Erin upstairs to my old bedroom, and she stood by the closet, holding the cardboard box I'd grabbed while I tossed a bunch of old, outdated clothes into it.

"If you want any of those midcalf Capri pants, circa 2002, knock yourself out," I teased when I noticed Erin checking out the things I was throwing into the box.

Erin was much taller than me, so the pants would never fit her. Plus, I didn't think the always-stylish Agent Lenehan was all that interested in my early 2000s-style garments—clothes I'd worn in high school—but it was fun to kid around some and lighten the mood.

"Uh, beautiful as they are"—Erin coughed—"I think I'll pass."

I laughed and said, "Good decision."

Soon, the box was full. "Do you think it's been about twenty minutes?" I asked Erin.

"Yeah, we can go now."

When we reached the top of the stairs, I remembered something. I paused and said to Erin, "Oh, can you wait here a minute."

I ran to my father's bedroom and grabbed a small overnight bag. I threw a change of clothes into the bag, for when my father was rescued. I also added a pair of his pajamas and a few toiletries. Adam had informed me my father would be brought to the rental home if the rescue attempt was successful. Dad wouldn't be returning to this house until round-the-clock protection was in place.

As we left the house, Erin offered to carry the box of clothes I'd gathered while I held onto the bag with my dad's things.

Suddenly, I had an idea.

"I don't want to just throw away those old clothes." I nodded to the box Erin was carrying as we walked to the car. "Do you mind if we drop those off at the Goodwill store on the way back?"

"No, not at all," Erin replied. "In fact, that gives us another opportunity to make sure you're seen."

It was decided, so we made a quick stop at the Goodwill store in town. And it was when I returned to the car—after turning in the box of clothes—that Erin got the call we'd all been waiting for.

"Ruslan made contact," she told me after she disconnected.

"What does that mean exactly?" I asked as I belted myself in.

"The plan's in motion, Maddy. Stowe and Adam set up a time to meet with Ruslan."

My hands shook as I started the ignition. "So, when is this all happening? When are they meeting?"

"Tonight."

Chapter Nine

"Promise me you'll be careful?" I placed my hands on Adam's chest. His skin was so warm, the muscles beneath so solid.

It was six in the evening and Adam and I were upstairs in the bedroom of the Harbour Falls rental. Adam, Stowe, Nate, and Max were scheduled to leave to meet with Ruslan in an hour.

Of course, Ruslan expected Adam and Stowe only. And even though the Adam-for-my-father trade was just a cover, to me, this whole plan still felt like Stowe was offering up Adam for a slaughter.

A chill ran down my spine at that horrible thought, and I reminded myself—again and again—that Stowe wasn't really trading Adam for my father. It was only part of the ruse for the guys to get close enough to Ruslan to kill him. And though I trusted Stowe—to a point—it comforted me to know Nate and Max would also be on hand, albeit in background roles.

Adam covered my hands with his and lowered them to my sides. "Maddy, everything will be fine. Besides the four of us, there will be agents nearby, including Erin. They'll step in, if needed."

I wasn't all that reassured seeing as the trained agents wouldn't exactly be in the thick of things. Still, I was compelled to ask, "How many agents will be available to you if you need them?"

Adam turned to face the dresser, while I sat down on the edge of the bed.

"I don't know," Adam said as he shrugged on a bulletproof vest. "Not too many or it will attract attention."

I started to protest, but Adam shot me a look in the mirror above the dresser that made me decide not to press the issue. So instead, I watched as Adam buttoned up a dark dress shirt over the bulletproof vest he'd just slipped on.

"Maybe you should stay here," I threw out.

I was grasping at straws, but it was worth a try.

"There's not really going to be a trade tonight, right?" I continued when Adam didn't respond. "Why put yourself in danger?"

Adam's back was to me, but he glanced up in the mirror again, his eyes meeting mine in the reflection. I smiled tightly, and Adam smiled back. His smile never reached his eyes, though.

"I have to go, Madeleine." Adam exhaled loudly. "You know I'm still part of the Wickingham Way project, and this is what's required of me. Besides, I don't want any fuck-ups when we get your father out of there."

I nodded, accepting Adam's words and his decision. I knew better than to ask where specifically my father was being held. But that didn't mean I wasn't insanely curious. I guessed a part of me wanted to know so I could potentially follow Adam and the others. In the past, I would have done so in a heartbeat.

But it seemed everyone was on to me these days. All the Wickingham Way players knew I'd been impulsive in the past, and, consequently, no one had divulged much of any-thing. The most I'd been told was that my dad was being held in an abandoned warehouse somewhere.

The only warehouse area I knew of was over in Harbourtown, the neighboring town to Harbour Falls.

I'd spent my share of time in Harbourtown while inves-tigating the Harbour Falls Mystery. Billy's, a rundown bar, was located in the heart of the warehouse district, where Chelsea Hannigan, Adam's ex-fiancée, once hung out on a regular basis. The clues I'd obtained from my visits to Billy's had led me to the truth of what had happened to Stowe's sister all those years ago. But I wouldn't have been able to uncover what turned out to be the most vital clue without the help of Jimmy, a young kid who had bartended at Billy's back in the fall.

But Jimmy was dead now…kind of, sort of, because of me.

I was sitting, picking at a loose thread on the comforter, sad and lost in thought, when Adam stepped over to me. "Hey, hey," he said soothingly. He sat down next to me and wiped at a tear I hadn't even noticed had fallen. "What's wrong? I can tell these tears are from more than just you worrying about tonight."

Adam had grown to know me so well, so there was no point in keeping from him all the things that were wearing me down.

"It's just finally all catching up to me," I admitted as I wiped away a tear. "I was thinking about Jimmy."

Adam rolled his eyes, and I clutched his arm. "Adam, I feel responsible in some ways. If I hadn't involved the poor kid, he'd probably still be alive today."

Another tear escaped, and Adam swiped it from my cheek. He cupped my chin and urged me to meet his gaze.

"Listen, Maddy. You didn't kill Jimmy, Ami did. You can't blame yourself for the actions of someone else."

"But Adam, if I hadn't—"

He silenced me with his lips. I slanted my head, and our kiss deepened. Suddenly I couldn't get enough of Adam. Without breaking our kisses, he allowed me to push him back onto the bed. We were both wearing jeans, but I undid mine and tugged them down my legs. After that task was accomplished—albeit awkwardly—I straddled Adam and got to work on his jeans.

"Maddy," he breathed out raggedly, "we don't have much time."

"I know." Adam lifted his hips, and I slid his jeans down. "We can be quick, yeah?"

I didn't want to stop, and neither did Adam. I gathered as much when he offered no resistance. Instead, he leaned up and kissed me.

The men involved in tonight's rescue were to meet at Stowe's house shortly, but I could think of nothing but the guy beneath me. I needed him, physically. And judging from how hard he was under my hand, it seemed he needed me just as much, and in the same way.

Neither of us bothered to remove any additional clothing. Adam pushed his boxer briefs down just enough so I could settle my body back over his. With a snap, he tore away my silk panties and then shoved me down on him.

I hissed out a breath but welcomed the rough intrusion. I began to move immediately, sliding up and down his swollen length.

"Fuck, Maddy," he rasped.

Adam had hidden his own frustration and stress better than I had realized. But now he unleashed all of his own pent-up emotions. He flipped me over onto my back, while his fingers dug into my hips, and his teeth latched onto my neck. He thrust into me with fervor. And when he released into me, he was at just the right angle to bring me to climax along with him.

I cried out, mostly in pleasure but also in pain as his teeth sank deeper into the tender skin on my neck. Still, I had no complaints. Times like this, when Adam was raw and feral with me, were often the best. And this encounter was no exception.

Afterward, Adam rolled off of me and adjusted his boxers and jeans. He then wrapped me up in a blanket and kissed me lightly on the lips. "I'm sorry, Maddy." He leaned back and smoothed hair away from my forehead. "I didn't mean to be so rough with you again. It seems the past couple of times we've been together have been so..."

"Urgent?" I offered.

Adam nodded and began to apologize.

But I stopped him by placing my hand on the side of his cheek. I rubbed at the light stubble. "It's all good, Adam," I assured him. "I feel fine. I actually kind of like it when you let go like that. Couldn't you tell?"

I raised an eyebrow, and Adam suppressed a chuckle. "Yeah, I guess so." He shook his head. "I just don't want to ever hurt you somehow."

"I know, Adam. And I'd stop you if that ever started to happen."

"Promise?" he asked.

"Cross my heart."

We sealed our promise with a kiss, but then it was time for Adam to go.

As I heard the front door close, I curled up in the blanket and sent up a prayer that everything would go as smoothly as my relationship with Adam had been going lately.

Chapter Ten

A few hours later, as the midnight hour neared, I found myself downstairs in the living room, pacing like crazy.

I was sure the rescue attempt was well under way by now, but I couldn't shake the nagging feeling that something had gone wrong. Several hours had passed since I'd watch the guys leave Stowe's house, and since then I'd heard nothing from anyone.

Not a word.

Naturally, that was driving me crazy.

I continued to pace. And if I didn't quit soon I knew I'd probably wear a hole in the area rug beneath my feet. Dammit, I needed an update or something. But I couldn't call any of the guys' cells, I might interrupt something important. Erin's cell, though, was another story. She was close to the location of the meet but not anywhere near Ruslan.

As I found her number and hit *send*, I reasoned that maybe she had heard something.

Unfortunately, there was no answer.

"Ugh." I swore a few times, finally stopped pacing, and threw my cell onto the couch in defeat.

Standing in the middle of the living room, I considered my options.

After Adam had left, I'd thrown on a sweatshirt and sweat pants. So I was more or less dressed. Therefore, driving over to Harbourtown and trying to find this secret warehouse was always an option. I knew the guys had taken Stowe's car, and I was sure I'd recognize the nondescript white rental if I saw it parked somewhere.

I grabbed my car keys off the coffee table, intent on taking action, but then I reconsidered.

What if Adam returned while I was gone?

If he did come home, maybe my father would be with him. *Hopefully* my father would be with him. And I certainly didn't want to be out traipsing around over in Harbourtown—out on some wild goose chase—and miss welcoming my father back.

All I really wanted, when it came right down to it, was to see my dad again, to give him a hug. Just to know he was safe and out of danger would mean everything. Running out of the house and putting myself in harm's way wasn't the answer.

I sighed.

I supposed I was finally learning to make good decisions. With a second resigned exhale of air, I made one now. I set the keys back down on the coffee table and sat down on the sofa.

Just as my butt hit the cushions, the front door flew open. I jumped back up and raced to see who was coming in.

"Adam, Dad," I cried out, elated when I ran right into my two favorite men in the world.

My dad had been rescued!

I threw my arms around my father—just as I'd intended to—and held onto him tightly.

"Madeleine..." my father croaked, too choked with emotion to continue.

After a good minute or two of hugging my dad, I finally let go. I stepped back and looked him over. Mayor Fitch appeared no worse for wear. His face was more drawn than usual, and his suit looked like it had been worn for several days, but otherwise my dad appeared unharmed.

"You're really okay?" I asked as I ran my hands down the sides of his arms, the heavy wool suit jacket material rough beneath my fingers.

"I'm fine, sweetheart...thanks to Adam." His eyes, the same hazel shade as mine, slid to Adam.

I'd never seen so much gratitude in my father's eyes, especially directed at Adam Ward. I imagined my father must have been terrified, having been at the mercy of a criminal like Ruslan. Thank God he'd been rescued.

But my relief was short-lived.

When I glanced past my dad, Adam indicated with a motion of his hand that I should take my father upstairs. And quickly. I knew then something had gone wrong, something Adam didn't want to mention in front of my dad.

"Come on, Dad, let's get you upstairs," I said. "You can clean up and change clothes, and then you can get settled in one of the spare bedrooms."

My father said he had no other clothes to change into, but I explained that I'd packed some clothes and toiletries for him—in the hopes he'd be rescued—when Erin and I had been at the house. My dad thanked me and gave me another tight hug.

Once my dad was settled upstairs, I hurried back down to the entry area.

Stowe and Erin were coming in the front door when I reached the bottom step. But they were not alone. Erin and

Stowe were supporting a slumped-over and very wounded Max Cleary.

"Oh my God, what happened?" I asked in a rush of words, freezing in place at the base of the stairs.

Max was hunched over but conscious. I saw him wince in pain as Stowe shifted. My neighbor was bearing most of the large man's weight, while Erin was pressing a thick and heavy cloth to a bleeding wound on Max's side.

"What happened?" I asked again. "How was Max hurt?"

"He was shot," Adam replied before he turned away from me and took over for Erin.

"Let's take him to the kitchen," Adam said as he gingerly pressed the cloth to Max's wound, just as Erin had done.

Erin led the way to the kitchen, and everyone followed. When Stowe and Adam lowered Max carefully to a chair at the table, I stopped in the doorway.

Adam glanced over at me and asked me to get more towels. "And some kind of antiseptic," he added as I started to turn to go.

"Okay," I called back over my shoulder, already on my way to retrieve what was needed from the linen closet upstairs.

A few minutes later, once all the supplies were gathered, Erin began to work on treating Max's wound.

"I knew I should have come along to the warehouse," she said as she ripped away Max's shirt to reveal a nasty-looking wound. "I was no help six blocks away."

Adam told me later it had been Stowe who'd insisted Erin stay out of direct danger. That was why she'd stationed herself in a car six blocks away from the warehouse. It was fairly obvious Stowe Hannigan was falling hard for Agent Lenehan.

I watched now as Stowe, at Erin's right side, handed her various medical implements as she asked for them. I had to concede the two of them worked well together.

While Erin and Stowe continued to administer care to Max, Adam stepped back to get out of their way. In doing so, he ended up standing next to me by the counter.

"Will Max be all right?" I asked quietly.

Adam nodded, his eyes remaining on the man who wasn't just his security guy but his dear friend as well.

"It's just a flesh wound," Adam said distractedly. "A bullet grazed him."

"Shouldn't he be seen by a physician, though?"

"Erin's had adequate training. She can handle it."

When I again expressed concern that Max should be seen by a doctor, Adam rolled his eyes. "Maddy, we can't just wheel him into a hospital. There'd be questions, you know, and authorities would surely be notified."

He shook his head as if I should have considered all of this before asking such an inane question.

Perhaps I should have, but I had not. I almost replied with a snarky comment, but it was clear Adam wasn't in a very good mood, which told me something more than Max getting shot had transpired.

Despite his dark mood, I still longed to throw my arms around the man I loved. I wanted to tell him how relieved I was that he'd returned unscathed, unlike poor Max. And I wanted to thank him for rescuing my father. But I sensed now was not the time to smother the man with adoration.

While Erin and Stowe attended to Max, who was looking more coherent with every passing minute, Adam slipped off the leather jacket he was wearing and unholstered his gun.

When he began to unbutton his shirt, I asked, "What are you doing?"

"Getting this bulletproof vest off," he responded as he slipped his shirt over his shoulders, tossed it to the counter, and removed the vest. "It's heavy as fuck."

In his state of undress, I couldn't help but admire Adam's smooth chest, his taut abs, and the sexy *v* of his tapered waist. I even caught Erin sneaking a quick peek. I couldn't blame her. Adam Ward really was an incredibly hot man.

And he was mine. I sometimes had to remind myself of my good fortune.

Adam grabbed up his shirt and slipped it back on, his motions fluid. He must have felt my eyes on him as he buttoned up his shirt, for he glanced over at me from under his long, black lashes. When a swath of jet-black hair fell to his forehead, I reached over and smoothed it back.

Adam gave me a smile that unfortunately didn't reach his eyes. And I knew then that Ruslan had gotten away. This was what was troubling Adam. He didn't have to say it out loud; I *knew*.

Which meant Adam was still in danger...and I was still in danger.

Hell, just about everyone we knew could be targeted by Ruslan. If anything, the fallen crime boss would be angrier than ever now that my father had been snatched away with relative ease, Max's injury notwithstanding.

Suddenly remembering that Nate had gone along on tonight's mission, I asked Adam where he was.

"He went back over to the island to get Helena," Adam said. "They're going to stay in the safe house until Ruslan is neutralized. They're leaving tonight."

That sounded like a good idea, especially now that the couple was expecting a child.

Worried, I asked Adam, "Ruslan doesn't know Helena's pregnant, does he?"

"No, I don't think so."

Adam didn't sound entirely sure, and I sensed from his dour expression that he was as worried as I.

Hell, a pregnant Helena would be a far better hostage than my father. Not only would Nate lay down his life for his wife and unborn child, but Adam would definitely jeopardize his safety as well to save Helena. The friendship between the three of them went back far and ran deep.

"How safe is that safe house?" I asked.

Adam didn't answer, and Stowe and Erin, who had apparently been listening to my conversation with Adam, glanced over at us.

I asked my question once more but directed it to Stowe and Erin.

Stowe said he didn't know, and Erin shrugged her shoulders. "Guess we'll find out," she said.

I found that response far from reassuring.

Chapter Eleven

L ater that same night, after Stowe and Erin had taken Max next door to Stowe's house to get some rest, I checked in on my father. I was hoping to talk with him and make sure he was truly all right, but I found him sleeping soundly.

I carefully closed the door to the spare bedroom and returned to the room I shared with Adam. The gorgeous Mr. Ward lay on his side, his broad-shouldered back facing me. The sheet rested just at his hip, but I couldn't discern whether he was wearing anything beneath it. Adam usually slept nude, and I assumed tonight was no exception. But I had no plans to start anything physical, not with my dad right down the hall.

I tried to be quiet, but when Adam heard me tiptoeing around, he rolled onto his back.

In the bedroom, lit only by slivers of moonlight streaming through the blinds, Adam appeared contrite. He ran his hand down his face and said, "I'm sorry I was short with you earlier."

I peeled off my sweatpants but kept my sweatshirt and panties on. Maneuvering my bra out of my sleeves, I tossed the lacy material to the floor and then crawled into bed next to Adam.

Since I was trying to behave myself, I was careful to keep my hands above Adam's waist, even as I wound an arm across his body.

Adam chuckled when he realized what I was doing. He lowered my hand so I could feel the waistband of his boxer briefs. "You don't have to keep your hands above the sheet, Maddy," he said softly. "I kind of figured with your dad here it'd be wise if we both remained at least partially clothed."

I snickered. "Good thinking."

We both laughed a little, and it felt good to joke around. With my dad safe, my mood felt lighter than it had in days.

"Thank you for saving my father," I whispered to Adam.

He turned onto his side so we were face-to-face. "Maddy..." He reached out and trailed his fingers down my cheek. "I love you, and I'd do anything for you. You know that, right?"

I did, so I nodded. And that was the point where something passed between us, some unspoken pledge that *this* was forever. I leaned in close enough to press my lips to his, and we kissed for the next few minutes.

It wasn't kissing designed to lead to something more; it was just a communion of lips and tongues that expressed our growing commitment to one another.

When we finally broke apart, we resumed our face-to-face positions on the pillows.

As I combed my fingers through Adam's silky, raven locks, I asked, "So, what happened tonight? How did Ruslan get away?"

Adam took a deep breath, and proceeded to tell me the story.

When the four guys had arrived at the warehouse, it felt to all of them as if something was off. The surrounding area was far too desolate, and the associate of Ruslan's who was supposed to meet Stowe and Adam out front was nowhere to be found.

Nate and Max, who were staying out of sight, conducted a quick sweep of the exterior of the building. Adam and Stowe, meanwhile, climbed up a fire escape along the side of the building that led them to the uppermost floor. The new vantage point gave them a bird's-eye view of the area surrounding the warehouse.

Still, there was still no sign of anyone. Adam and Stowe agreed that was odd. But nothing appeared blatantly amiss.

Adam suggested stepping into the warehouse, as there was a heavy metal door at the top of the fire escape. Stowe, though, was hesitant. Since there seemed to be no need for Nate and Max to remain hidden, Adam texted and told them to meet him and Stowe at the top of the fire escape.

Adam wanted their opinion on what their next move should be—go in or wait.

Not much was decided once Nate and Max arrived, as the four men got in to a heated debate.

"Stowe and Max thought it could've been a setup," Adam explained. "So, there was talk of turning around and leaving, or sending me back to the car. But there was no way I was leaving without first checking to see if your father was in that warehouse."

Even though I knew the story ended well, I still shuddered. When he noticed, Adam banded his arm around my back and pulled me close to him.

"What happened?" I asked.

"Max tried the door and it was unlocked, so the four of us went in."

Adam explained that from that high up, they had a complete view of the warehouse interior. It was empty...except for a man tied to chair in the center of the ground floor. The captive man's eyes were covered by a blindfold.

That man was my father. And my dad was being guarded by a man with a gun, but the man was not Ruslan.

Before anyone knew what was happening, the man with the gun glanced up to the catwalk five stories up. Soon as he saw Adam, he took a shot at him.

Luckily, he missed. But the stray bullet grazed Max, which was how Adam's personal security guy had ended up injured.

The man made a run for it, his interest in guarding my dad no longer a top priority.

But he didn't make it far. Stowe stopped him cold when he raised his gun and fired, killing the man.

"Jeez, Stowe sure is lethal," I interjected.

Adam just nodded and then continued his explanation of the events that followed.

Stowe helped the injured and bleeding Max outside and back down the fire escape, while Adam made a call to Erin. He directed her to meet them outside the warehouse as soon as possible.

"So, my dad didn't see that Max had been injured?"

"No, he was still down on the ground floor, bound and blindfolded. We didn't want to make things any worse for him once we reached him. So after we made sure Stowe got Max to Erin, Nate and I went back in the building and rescued your dad." Adam paused and blew out a breath. "Your dad was so shaken. He'd heard the shots, and he knew Ruslan's minion had been killed, but he had no idea Max had been shot as well."

I appreciated the thoughtfulness toward my traumatized father and told Adam as much.

"I just wish he'd not been dragged into this at all," Adam continued. "The mayor is a good man. I'm sorry this happened to him, Maddy."

Adam appeared distraught, but I didn't hold anything against him. Hell, I felt guilty for knowing I was the one who *should* have been taken.

"Hey," I began. "I'm just glad everyone is okay. I mean, I know Max is hurt, but he'll recover." Sighing, I added, "God, I don't know what I would have done if either you or my dad had ended up hurt like that."

I ran my hand along Adam's shoulder and trailed down his arm, slowly and carefully, like I was searching for some invisible injury.

Adam cupped my cheek and kissed my lips. "Your father is safe now, Maddy."

"Yeah, but are you?" I questioned, searching his stormy blue eyes for an answer.

Adam didn't respond, but his darkened gaze said it all. He wouldn't be safe until Ruslan was out of the picture... for good.

And that meant I was still in as much danger as Adam.

Chapter Twelve

Since Adam had business to attend to with Stowe the next day—something to do with getting Max back over to Fade Island safely—I was on my own. So I decided to spend some time with my father.

After having come so close to losing him, I wanted to spend whatever time I could with my dad. And though I'd asked him to stay with me at the Victorian rental house for a while longer, the stubborn mayor insisted on returning to his own home.

Really, there was no reason for him not to. The extra security was in place, so Dad would be well protected.

I still hoped he'd reconsider, stay with me for maybe a week or two, but there was no stopping my dad once he made up his mind. So stubborn, that man.

Not that *I* was ever that way…

Ha, who was I kidding? I was my father's daughter, through and through. So I gave up on arguing with Dad. After we ate breakfast, I drove him to his house.

My dad was chatty on the drive there, but when we stepped into the living room, my father, who'd seemingly been running on adrenaline all morning, deflated a bit.

With a deep breath and subsequent loud exhale, Dad sank down into the cushions on the sofa.

"God, I missed this place," he said as he glanced around. "I thought I'd never see home again." His eyes then settled on me, sadness brewing in his hazel gaze. "But my real fear, sweetheart, was that I'd never see *you* again."

"Oh, Dad."

Choked up, I went to my father. I sat down next to him on the sofa and hugged him.

"I was so afraid for you," I murmured. "I'm so sorry. You shouldn't have been dragged into this mess. Adam feels badly, too. He—"

My father leaned back and shushed me. "Madeleine, I want no more apologies, not from you or from Adam. Neither of you did anything wrong. And you can stop hiding things from me too. I know Adam is in more danger than either of you are letting on. I may be getting older, but don't think I can't see the fear on everyone's faces, especially on yours and Adam's."

I didn't have the heart to tell my dad how very right he was, but I also didn't deny his observations. What I did try to do was distract him from the troubles he needn't be worrying about.

"Hey, are you hungry for lunch?" I asked, effectively changing the subject. "I can make us something."

My father admitted he was famished, as he'd not been given much in the way of food while being held captive.

We moved to the kitchen, and while I got to work on boiling some water to toss spaghetti noodles into, my dad loosened the lid on a jar of pasta sauce.

A short while later, Dad and I sat down at the kitchen table and dug into hearty bowls of spaghetti.

We chatted about nothing of consequence, until, at one point, my dad started to reminisce. He loved to do that from time to time. Some of the stuff I tuned out—I'd heard most of his old stories—but when he began rattled off a rather interesting tale, one that involved a much-younger Adam, I perked up considerably.

"I have to admit, Maddy," Dad mused, "I always suspected Adam Ward had more than a passing interest in you."

"Oh, really?" I twirled a forkful of pasta on a spoon. "What made you think that?"

"Well," Dad continued, "years ago, Adam showed his hand, so to speak. He was attending a fundraiser here in Harbour Falls with his dad." My dad waved his hand. "Some political event in my honor or some such thing."

I set down my utensils. "Wait...I've never heard this story."

And I had not. Jeez, had everyone known of Adam's secret high school crush on me but me? How could I have been so clueless?

"So, tell me the story. What happened at the fundraiser? Don't leave anything out, Dad."

My father chuckled. "Calm down, Maddy. Let me tell you the story from the beginning."

I quieted, as Dad had asked, and after a few seconds, he continued, "So, as I said, this was ages ago. The event was in the city hall ballroom. Lots of important townsfolk were in attendance. And that, of course, included Adam's father, Dr. Ward. You'll remember he was the dean of our local college back then."

I nodded. "When was this exactly?" I asked, curious as to the time frame of this fundraiser.

My father seemed to consider. "Hmm, I'd be inclined to say all this occurred at the end of your senior year in high school, probably around April or May of that year."

"Oh, okay."

"Anyway, when I had the chance to talk with Dr. Ward for an extended period of time, young Adam was at his side. Dr. Ward had asked Adam to accompany him so he could show him how political business is conducted." My father took a sip from his glass of water. "At one point, Dr. Ward and I were in the midst of discussing how I planned to renovate some of the older Harbour Falls landmarks. That's when a call came in for Dr. Ward. He excused himself so he could go to another room to take the call in private."

"Didn't Adam leave with him?" I asked.

"No, not right away, Maddy. Dr. Ward motioned for Adam to follow, but he told his dad he'd be along in a minute. There was something he wanted to ask me."

Ooh, this is getting interesting. "And what was that?" I asked.

My father smiled knowingly. "After his father left the room, Adam cleared his throat, like he was gathering his courage or something. Then he asked me if you were in attendance that evening."

Damn, I remembered that fundraiser now. I'd blown it off, thinking it'd be boring as hell. I recalled that I had hung out with J.T. and Ami that night. We'd gone to a completely forgettable movie. What a shame!

"Did you ever find out why Adam was asking if I was there?" I ventured.

My father paused, continued to smile knowingly, and said quietly, "I sure did. Adam told me he wanted to ask you to save a dance for him."

Oh my.

Even all these years later, my pulse raced. Adam Ward at eighteen had been almost as good as present-day, twenty-eight-year-old Adam Ward. He was more lean back then but just as athletic. Maybe even more so, seeing as, at the time, he was the star receiver on our high school football team.

I sighed wistfully, imagining how gorgeous Adam must have looked that night, all dressed to the nines in a black tux and tie. But then I remembered a less-than-pleasant fact from long ago. Adam had been wrapped up with Chelsea Hannigan throughout his high school years. *Ugh.*

I made a face and asked my dad, "But wasn't Chelsea with Adam that night?"

My dad shook his head. "No, no. Not that I recall. Adam was there alone with his father. And"—Dad's eyes met mine—"I must say, he appeared quite upset when he learned you weren't at the party."

"So, no Chelsea," I mused out loud, "interesting."

I tried to remember all the gossip from back then. I did recall a short window of time where Adam and Chelsea had broken up. I mentally kicked myself again for not having attended that stupid fundraiser. Perhaps my relationship with Adam would have kindled from a flicker to a flame that very night. If he'd been upset that I wasn't there, as my father had just said, then maybe that fundraiser event would have marked the beginning of our story.

Alas… It saddened me to think ten years that Adam and I could have been together were forever lost.

My father seemed to sense what I was thinking. He reached across the table and placed his hand over mine. "Madeleine, I didn't tell you that story to make you sad. I told you so you'd know Adam had feelings for you, even back then." My dad sighed. "These past few months, Maddy, I have to admit there were times, especially in the beginning, when I found it difficult to accept your relationship with Adam. I didn't always trust his intentions. Men that powerful…" Dad trailed off.

"Dad, Adam's intentions are true. I promise."

"Oh, Maddy, I know that now. I don't doubt that Adam loves you tremendously."

"Adam does love me," I agreed. "It's just all this other stuff that worries me now."

"Like the Wickingham Way fallout?" my dad asked, a clear reference to Ruslan.

I nodded, and my father said in his most serious tone, "Listen, Maddy, whatever's happening with Ruslan, don't let it tear you and Adam apart."

"I won't, Dad," I promised. "This crap will all come to an end, and then Adam and I can finally focus on just our relationship. We're in this for the long run. Forever."

My dad smiled. Contented—I imagined—that his daughter had found her true love.

Forever, I whispered once more, feeling pretty darn contented myself.

Chapter Thirteen

A curious thing happened in the weeks following my father's rescue; Ruslan dropped off the radar.

It appeared as if the crime boss had disappeared, gone missing...maybe even been taken out for good. I had no idea, nor did Adam, although we hoped for the last option to be the one to hold true.

Stowe, who'd been a wealth of knowledge for a very long time, was unfortunately no longer much of a resource, especially when it came to figuring out where his old boss had slunk off to. Ruslan had cut off all contact with Stowe after realizing the man who'd once pledged his allegiance to the ruthless crime boss was now on the side of good.

Like Stowe, Erin—as well as the government entity she worked for—knew next to nothing. Things were at a standstill, at least in regard to Ruslan. His men, however, had begun to pop up, either through capture or by turning themselves in. One by one, the government thoroughly questioned each former member of the crime syndicate. The hope was to uncover some scrap of information regarding what had happened to the missing Ruslan.

But no one had any definitive answers.

There was, however, plenty of speculation that one of his own men had killed him, as he was not particularly liked or well-regarded. I sure as hell hoped the man who wanted Adam dead was no longer with us. But since nothing could be confirmed one way or the other, Adam and I remained merely cautiously optimistic.

Everyone involved with the Wickingham Way project—either directly or indirectly—felt pretty much the same way. All agreed Ruslan could have been taken out. As a result, Nate and Helena considered a return to Harbour Falls. Adam talked them out of it, though. He convinced our friends to remain at the safe house until confirmation could be made that Ruslan was indeed deceased.

Good call, I thought, *better safe than sorry.*

Adam and I discussed a move of our own, a return to Fade Island. But we elected to stay on at the Victorian rental house in Harbour Falls awhile longer. True, we were well into March, and spring had certainly sprung, early this year, incidentally. But we felt it prudent to push our timeline to return to the island back a bit. As with Helena and Nate, we, too, needed to know Ruslan was out of our lives forever before making our next move.

"Do you think he's dead?" I asked Adam one morning.

Adam had been outside, messing around in the front yard, readying Mrs. Heider's flower beds for spring. Apparently, Adam was very bored.

But also very sweet, I thought, as I observed the modest bouquet of tulips and crocuses he was carrying.

"Maddy..." Adam sighed as he handed me the bright magenta tulip and purple crocus bouquet. "I bring you flowers and my thoughtful gesture turns your thoughts to death." He held his hand to his heart, wounded. "Really, you're giving me a complex here."

I knew what Adam was doing—changing the subject to something other than Ruslan.

Still, I pressed on. "So, do you think he's dead?"

Adam shrugged his wide shoulders. "I don't know, Maddy..." His voice grew serious. "...perhaps."

I held tightly to my bouquet and wished for a more definitive answer than "perhaps."

Thankfully, not every day was spent ruminating over what may have happened to the head of the criminal organization Adam (and the government) had so unmercifully brought to its knees.

For instance, on a happier note, there was more than just spring in the air. Love was in the air as well. In fact, love was flourishing.

In my relationship with Adam, with all the secrets and mysteries finally behind us, I felt closer to him than I had at any time during our first six months together, except for maybe the days spent at the cabin. Those days had been amazing. And like those times, I still craved Adam's presence like crazy, basking in our every moment together.

Bottom line, things were awesome.

Another interesting development was that Adam and I weren't the only two ridiculously-in-love Harbour Falls residents.

Nope, not at all.

Seems Stowe and Erin's relationship had turned into something serious. So serious, in fact, that Erin had moved in with Stowe next door.

"Moving in?" I'd asked Erin when I caught her lugging boxes into Stowe's house one afternoon.

"Yeah," she'd said, balancing a cardboard carton on her hip. "I know this seems fast, but with the life Stowe and I lead, you learn to seize the moment."

I wasn't sure how to respond to that comment, so I'd just nodded and watched Erin proceed into the Victorian next to mine.

I'd thought with Ruslan seemingly out of the picture, Stowe would leave Harbour Falls. But no, Stowe decided to stay in town awhile longer. Apparently he—and Erin, since she wasn't returning to Boston any too soon—also wanted to be sure Ruslan was no longer a threat.

I wasn't sure what it would be like living next door to Stowe and Erin, but it turned out to be a good thing. With them so close, Adam and I had an opportunity to get to know the two of them better as a couple. Before that happened though, Adam and Stowe had needed to reach a longer-than-twenty-four-hour truce. Thankfully, they did, and that made life easier for everyone.

I had once believed I'd never see true peace between the two hard-headed men, but I guessed Stowe gunning down the man who'd taken a shot at Adam at the warehouse went a long way in convincing Adam that Stowe was firmly entrenched on our side.

And thus began our friendship with Stowe and Erin.

To my surprise, as Adam and I began to spend more and more time with the couple—going out to dinner, catching a few movie, visiting each other's homes—I discovered I genuinely liked Agent Lenehan. Erin was funny and sweet, and she became a true friend over time. I learned early on that while she could indeed be a tough-as-nails federal agent, Erin was also a fun-loving person who was easy to hang out with.

And that is how one sunny March afternoon I found myself walking with Erin in the quaint and tidy downtown area of Harbour Falls. We'd just had lunch at an awesome

Mexican restaurant in town and were heading back to my car.

Suddenly, Erin slowed.

"Is everything okay?" I asked, slowing up on the sidewalk next to her.

She waved her hand. "Oh, yeah, I didn't mean to scare you. I just remembered there's something I need to pick up at the jewelry store. Do you mind if we stop in there for a minute? It won't take long."

"No, no, that's fine," I replied. "I don't mind at all."

It was a nice afternoon and there was no reason to rush home, so we turned and headed in the direction of the jewelers.

As we walked, Erin explained why she needed to stop in the jewelry store.

"I dropped a necklace off last week. I broke the damn clasp somehow. Anyway, I can't believe I almost forgot it's supposed to be ready today. Stowe and I are going out tonight, and I'd really love to wear it with the outfit I have planned. Sorry I didn't think of it sooner, Maddy."

I assured her, again, that the detour was no problem.

The jeweler was right next to city hall, and I knew my dad was working today. Dad was fully recovered from his kidnapping ordeal, but I hadn't been able to truly rest easy knowing Ruslan could still be out there somewhere. That concern led me to check in on my father quite often. And since we were right here at city hall, I asked Erin, "Would it be all right if we stopped in to say hi to my dad before we hit the jewelry store?"

"Sure, Maddy," Erin replied with a smile. "Your dad is such a sweetheart. I always enjoy seeing him."

I chuckled, since my dad loved to see the people who had saved his life just as much. He never failed to thank the

Wickingham Way participants profusely every time he ran into one of them.

Today turned out to be no exception.

In my father's office, Dad grabbed up Erin's hand and shook it vigorously. "Thank you again, young lady," he said. "I don't mean to keep repeating myself, but I just can't thank you enough for all you did to rescue me."

Erin *pshaw*-ed, "Aw, Mayor Fitch, that's so nice of you to say. But—like I told you before—you give me entirely too much credit. Really, your rescue was all Stowe and Adam's doing. And Nate and Max helped, of course. But me, I wasn't even at the warehouse."

"I know, I know," my father replied. "But you were close by the whole time, ready to help. And I know you were instrumental in setting up the whole rescue. For all those things, I thank you."

Erin accepted my father's gratitude graciously. Dad, who had somehow gotten wind that Max had been shot during the rescue attempt, turned to me. "That reminds me, Maddy, how is Max faring?"

"Recovering well," I said, echoing what I'd recently been told by Adam.

Erin nodded in agreement. "That's what I've heard, as well, Mayor Fitch. Max is doing great."

"Excellent, excellent, that makes me happy to hear."

We sat and talked for a while longer, but then my dad's secretary called and reminded him he had a town council meeting to attend to down the hall.

"I almost forgot," he said into the receiver, before hanging up with his secretary.

Dad got up and hugged us both. And then we said our farewells.

Erin and I made our way to our next stop, the jewelry store.

As we stepped into the store, the little bell above the door to alert the staff to someone's presence jingled. Erin, who was telling me more of her and Stowe's plans tonight, continued chattering away, even as my attention was drawn to a good-looking man at the counter, signing what looked like a receipt.

But wait, I knew the guy.

"Adam?" I exclaimed.

Why is Adam at a jewelry store?

Adam glanced my way, raising an eyebrow. "What are you doing here, Maddy?"

I could tell I'd caught him completely off guard, but I gave him points for trying to play it cool.

"Why are you here?" I blurted out, not bothering to answer the same question he'd just posed to me.

Adam's silence spoke volumes, as did the withering look he gave me. He was up to something, but he wasn't about to divulge a thing.

My suspicions were confirmed when the lady behind the counter, who'd not paid us any heed up to this point, attempted to hand Adam what looked like a black velvet ring box.

Adam quickly turned away from the woman, effectively blocking my view.

"Madeleine," he purred, still so cool, collected, and smooth as he leaned back against the counter. "I knew you were coming into town today for lunch, but I don't recall you making any mention of a stop to the jewelers."

"Uh—"

"We're here for me," Erin piped in. "I'm here to pick up a necklace."

Adam's gaze moved to Erin. He eyed her meaningfully for several seconds, and then Erin turned to me and
amended, "Actually, um, I think I was mistaken, Maddy.
The necklace won't be ready until tomorrow."

Yeah, right.

Clearly, Adam wanted me out of the store, and Erin was
going to make sure that happened. All of this was fine with
me because I'd seen the ring box. And if it meant what I
thought it meant, then the incredibly handsome Adam
Ward was planning to propose. To me. And probably not
too far off in the future.

Oh. My. God. Could I have been any happier? Abso-
freaking-lutely not.

I resisted the urge to squeal in joy, and instead I waved
a light and airy farewell to Adam, all while allowing Erin to
usher me back out the door.

"Holy crap!" I exclaimed once we were outside the store
and standing at the curb.

Erin must have seen the box as well, as she glanced
away and said nothing. But I caught her sly smile.

Had Adam confided in her? Had she known his plans
for today? Maybe, but I doubted it. She never would have
suggested stopping in at the jewelry store had she thought
Adam would be there.

Still, curious as I was, I longed to ask Erin if she knew
anything—anything at all—of Adam's plans.

Of course, I did no such thing. Adam's intention was
for whatever he had planned to remain a secret. And I'd
learned to respect those types of secrets. So I quelled my
curiosity and moved the conversation to things unrelated to
jewelry stores, things unrelated to rings, things unrelated to
possibilities of proposal.

Erin relaxed, noticeably so, when she realized I wasn't going to beg her for answers or try to find out what she knew of Adam's intentions. She and I walked back to the car, chatting amiably of other things. But I didn't pay too much attention to the mundane subjects we discussed.

How could I? I was too elated, too full of joy.

Adam had apparently not been joking around back at the cabin last month. It appeared as if the gorgeous Mr. Ward truly wanted to spend the rest of his life with me.

I sighed, contented. Erin didn't notice; she kept right on talking.

It didn't matter, as all I could think of was Adam and the impending proposal. I wanted the same things as Adam—to get married, to spend the rest of our lives together. And I couldn't wait to get started on this future of ours.

Too bad the past always has a way of catching up to you.

Chapter Fourteen

Hours after catching Adam in the jewelry store—signing a receipt for something contained within a black velvet ring box—I was flying high.

Adam is going to propose, I singsonged to myself as I finished making dinner.

I pictured how it all might go down as I plated grilled chicken breasts.

I imagined Adam getting down on bended knee and asking me to marry him. A flurry of excitement coursed through me. Would Adam wine and dine me first? Would he whisk me away to somewhere exotic and then propose?

The possibilities were endless and I couldn't begin to guess, but a part of me kind of hoped he'd keep it simple. I liked the old-fashioned bended-knee part of things, but I had no need for fancy foods or exotic locales as a preface to a proposal from the man I loved. Adam's presence alone was enough to impress me. Additionally, some of the best times spent with my guy were ones where we just hung out together, totally relaxed and being ourselves.

I poured a white wine Adam had brought over from his collection on Fade Island. And as I set the bottle on the table, I heard the man I was always thinking of opening the front door.

Adam was home.

Since I wasn't supposed to have seen the velvet ring box, I pushed all thoughts of proposal from my mind. Putting on my best poker face, I busied myself with straightening the flatware at the place settings on the table.

"Hey, beautiful," Adam said as he strode into the kitchen, looking as debonair as when I'd caught him earlier in the jewelry store.

He was still dressed in the same exquisitely tailored, charcoal gray suit, and, damn, the man was *gorgeous*.

I turned back to the flatware in an effort to stay on task, but when I felt Adam come up behind me, I leaned back into his powerful chest.

"Adam," I murmured, closing my eyes and letting myself go as I inhaled his delightfully masculine scent.

Trailing tender kisses along my neck, he asked huskily, "Can dinner wait?"

I spun so we were facing one another. Adam cupped my face in his hands, and I nodded into his warm fingers that yes, dinner could definitely wait. The chicken breasts could easily be reheated, and the salad I'd prepared as an accompaniment would stay fresh for hours.

With a sexy smirk, Adam leaned down and kissed me fully on the mouth. Neither of us mentioned the jewelry store. In fact, we did very little talking at all. Adam scooped me up in his capable arms and carried me up to the bedroom.

Clothes were hastily discarded, and foreplay was quick and frantic, but as Adam pushed me back onto the bed, he slowed our hungry and needy groping.

"I love you, Maddy," he whispered as he held my gaze and entered me slowly.

Slowly, but so fucking skillfully.

I moaned on a particularly toe-curling stroke and murmured my own declaration of love. Our love-making continued, until we found release. Afterward, I lay in Adam's arms, blissed out and happy. But I sensed Adam was distracted, distracted in a way that had nothing to do with my having run in to him in the jewelry store.

"Is everything all right?" I asked as I snuggled deeper into his hold.

Adam glanced down at me, and in a far from light-hearted tone, he said, "Maddy, I didn't want to mention it earlier, but I received word a few hours ago that Ruslan was spotted not far from Harbour Falls."

Ah, now things made sense.

No wonder Adam had been so ready to get physical with me. Danger always heightened our desire for one another. But this was bad news.

I swallowed hard. This meant Ruslan was alive.

"Where was he seen?" I softly queried.

Adam twined his fingers in my hair. "West of Harbour Falls, leaving Harbourtown."

Shit. "That's less than an hour away from here," I lamented.

"I know," Adam whispered.

"Who spotted him? And how'd he get away?"

I exhaled harshly when Adam shared with me that the agent who'd spotted Ruslan had been shot when he tried to approach the dangerous man.

"Oh my God." I sat up abruptly, and the sheet covering me fell to my waist. "Is the agent okay? It wasn't Erin, was it?"

Adam coaxed me back down to him. "No, it wasn't Erin, Maddy." My heart beat wildly as I laid my head on his shoulder.

"And yes, the agent who was shot will be okay. But I think, all things considered, we should relocate."

I looked up at Adam. "Again? Do we have to?"

It felt as if I'd spent the past few months settling into new places, only to be uprooted time and time again.

Adam smiled sadly. "I'm afraid so, Maddy."

I sighed, resigned. "Back to the safe house, then?"

Adam confirmed that the safe house was our best option.

Trying to remain positive, I said, "Well, at least Helena and Nate are still there. That'll be fun. I'm sure they're getting bored out there all by themselves."

"Yeah," Adam distractedly agreed. "I know Nate and Helena will be glad to see us. I'll make arrangements for Stowe or Erin to drive us out this weekend. I think Ruslan will be laying low for the time being, so we should be fine here in Harbour Falls for a few more days. That'll give us time to pack."

"What about Stowe and Erin?" I asked. "Will they be okay staying here in town?"

Adam chuckled. "Maddy, Stowe and Erin are both trained assassins. They'll be fine."

Interesting…

I knew Stowe was an assassin, but this was the first I'd heard that Erin was trained as such as well. Sure, Agent Lenehan was a force to be reckoned with—I never doubted that—but I just didn't picture her as being *that* lethal.

"I thought Erin was just an agent for the government?" I asked Adam.

He smoothed back my hair. "She is, Madeleine. Let's just say Agent Lenehan is a very well-trained agent."

"How well trained?" I whispered.

"Very."

Well, that was vague. But I didn't question Adam any further. Hell, I'd already been made privy to loads of classified information. I was satisfied with that. I really didn't care for details on how many "hits" funny and sweet Erin had under her belt.

But wow, I had to say, I sure felt safe knowing all these well-trained, deadly individuals had my back.

Yeah, I felt safe, secure, and protected.

Turns out, I wasn't any of those things.

Chapter Fifteen

The night before Adam and I planned to leave for the safe house—*back to the deep woods of Maine,* I thought—I felt... uneasy.

Sure, everything was packed and ready to go. And arrangements had been made for Stowe to drive us out to the safe house early Saturday morning. So I should have felt okay with things. There was something nagging at me, though, some sense of foreboding. Passing it off as the jitters from having to pick up and move again, I dismissed my bad feeling.

Just settle down, Maddy, I thought to myself as I hunkered down in the living room and contented myself with waiting for Adam to return home. But that didn't work out very well, since, as usual, Adam was running late.

Adam had gone over to Fade Island earlier in the day to take care of some island-related business with Max. Max was recovering nicely from the gunshot wound he'd sustained but not quite enough to resume his duties of keeping Adam Ward safe and sound. Consequently, until Max was back to 100 percent, he was picking up some light duties and filling in for the absent Nate Jackson by taking care of the day-to-day island business and all that entailed.

Why Adam needed to venture over to the island today, I had no clue. Fade Island business was generally not all that pressing. But when I thought about it more and more, I concluded I actually did have a small inkling as to why Adam needed to go to the island. I'd overheard him talking on the phone a few nights earlier, and he'd been speaking to Max about renovating the old lighthouse located at the southeastern tip of the island. I heard Adam utter words like *repaint* and *restore*, so I was fairly certain he was having the tall structure renovated.

A further tip-off as to what Adam's plans were had been a conversation he'd started with me last night. Adam had asked me what my thoughts were on the lighthouse.

"Do you want it torn down, Maddy?" he'd questioned. Then he'd added, "'Cause if that's the case, then it can certainly be arranged."

"God, no," I'd replied. "The lighthouse is a landmark, Adam. You can't destroy it. It's been there since Fade Island was first settled."

"I know, Maddy, but..." Adam sighed. "After everything that's happened down there, I wasn't sure how you felt about it remaining."

True, Ami and Jennifer had trapped me in the lighthouse one night back in the fall, with the intention of offing me, just like they'd done to Chelsea Hannigan. But the things that had happened at the lighthouse on one awful night didn't color my overall opinion of the structure.

Truth be told, I actually loved the lighthouse. The lighthouse was where Adam had first attempted to kiss me, after we'd walked down from the café one foggy evening. Those good memories—the ones I held close to my heart—far outweighed any bad ones.

"Please don't tear it down," I'd pleaded with Adam.

He'd nodded thoughtfully, and then said, "Okay, it can stay. But I do have a plan."

"Oh, what's that?" I'd leaned in to Adam and nuzzled along his jaw.

Adam had taken the opportunity to distract me, and I found out nothing more that particular evening. But the phone conversation I'd overheard—and that single discussion with Adam—led me to believe he had gone over to Fade Island to get the lighthouse renovations kicked off.

The grandfather clock in the corner of Mrs. Heider's living room chimed. "Seven o'clock, damn," I mumbled to myself.

Adam was still not home.

"Ugh, I am so bored," I complained out loud as I leaned my head back on the sofa.

Just then my cell buzzed.

I glanced at the screen. *Adam. Thank God.*

"Where are you?" I asked without preamble.

Adam laughed. "That's how you answer the phone, Madeleine? I'm thinking someone must be feeling restless."

He knew me so well.

"I am," I confirmed. "Where are you?"

"Well, the ferry just docked down at Cove Beach. I should be home in less than an hour."

"Another hour?" I lamented, frustrated at the prospect of more downtime.

Then, I suddenly had a brainstorm. "Hey, what if I meet you in Harbour Falls? We can eat dinner in town. I didn't make anything here since I didn't know what time you'd be back. And you must be hungry, right? Lord knows I'm famished."

Adam chuckled a little and confirmed he was indeed hungry, but then he grew quiet. I knew he was probably about to veto my idea of eating out. He'd been especially protective of me the past few days, ever since news of Ruslan's reappearance near Harbourtown had surfaced. Adam was being so cautious, in fact, that I'd only been permitted to visit with Erin next door. Other than those couple of forays to my neighbor's abode, I'd remained holed up in the house. As a result, I was feeling more than a touch stir-crazy at the moment.

"Please, Adam," I pleaded when I sensed he was about to nix my proposal. "Nothing's going to happen. I'm sure Ruslan is staying as far away from this area as he can, especially after almost being apprehended."

Adam sighed and, to my delight, relented. "Okay, Maddy," he said, "but come straight to my Harbour Falls office. I'll meet you outside the front entrance in half an hour. We can decide where we want to eat then, all right?"

I happily agreed and disconnected with Adam. I grabbed up my car keys from the little table in the entry hall, and then I was off.

*

Adam was right where he said he'd be, waiting for me out in front of his Harbour Falls office. It was dark, though, and I couldn't be sure he saw me when I gave him a little wave. In any case, I felt sure he'd recognize my maroon BMW, especially when I parked close by. I was directly in front of his Escalade, in fact.

After I got out of my car and hit the lock button on the key fob, I took a moment to glance around and assess my surroundings. Having spent so much time lately around Adam, Stowe, and Erin, I found myself thinking these days much as they did—always assess the area you're in, check for threats, and remain on the lookout for irregularities.

If I'd been this savvy back when I was investigating the Harbour Falls mystery, I might not have made so many mistakes, or miscalculated so much. Maybe Jimmy would never have ended up dead; and then maybe I wouldn't have found myself under suspicion for murder. One thing for sure, I certainly would have never allowed myself to be duped by a forged note that resulted in me being trapped down at the lighthouse by two crazed women.

But those things were in the past. I'd learned a lot since then; I'd changed.

I blew out a breath and had just stepped away from the side of my car when a vehicle driving by—very slowly—drew my attention.

I quickly noted the details: large sedan, black-tinted windows. Not the kind of car that typically cruised down the streets of Harbour Falls on a Friday evening. I found it odd, yes, but I dismissed my concern when I heard Adam call out my name.

I tightened the belt on my jacket and hurried over to where Adam stood, waiting for me on the sidewalk. Adam was dressed casually—faded jeans and a dark green shirt. I had to smile. Typical Adam, he was still all hot and put together, even when dressed down.

I greeted my man with a chaste peck to the cheek that he, with a slant of his head, turned into a full-on kiss. Within seconds a steamy make-out session was underway. It didn't matter, as the streets of Harbour Falls were more or less empty. Sure, a few cars drove by, but most of the storefronts were dark, closed up for the night. Some of the intermittent restaurants and coffee shops were open and brightly lit, but the sidewalks around us were still empty.

I let out a little moan, and Adam pulled me close to his body, kissing me with abandon.

When our make-out session finally cooled to a simmer, Adam, arms still around me, leaned back. "Well, hello there, Madeleine."

"Hello back at you, Mr. Ward." I giggled, and added, "Guess we better go eat before we end up completely side-tracked, eh?"

"Probably a good idea." Adam nodded. "So where should we eat dinner? Have any suggestions?"

We began to walk to where the cars were parked. "Actually I do have a thought," I said. "Do you want to try out that new fusion-cuisine restaurant? I heard it's really good, and it's only a couple of blocks from here."

"That works for me," Adam replied as he unlocked the doors to his Escalade.

I paused at the curb. "We can just walk there, Adam. It's just a few roads over."

Adam frowned.

I knew he didn't like the idea of walking to the restaurant, leaving us exposed like that. But I hated the thought of climbing back into one of our vehicles.

"Please, Adam," I pressed. "It's such a nice evening for a walk."

After what appeared to be a moment of deliberation, Adam gave in. He snatched up my hand, and we started in the direction of the new restaurant.

"Thank you," I murmured as I leaned into him.

"Maddy, Maddy," he sighed.

Traffic was light, so when I caught sight of the same car—black sedan, tinted windows—that had driven by when I'd been parking my car I drew in a quick breath.

Adam glanced over at me. "Everything all right?" he questioned.

"I think so."

But I wasn't sure, so I asked, "Did you see that car before?" I pointed to the red taillights of the black sedan, now in the distance, as it turned onto a side road.

Adam squinted. "I don't think so," he replied. "Why?"

"Well, I saw a dark car exactly like that one right after I parked. I think it might have been the same car."

The ever-cautious Mr. Ward tensed. "Maddy, you should have said something right away. You know we have to be careful."

"I know…and I'm sorry."

Adam flipped up the snap of the holster that held in place the firearm at his waist. I didn't want to cause any undue concern, so I told Adam that though the two cars were similar, I couldn't be *completely* certain they were one and the same.

Still, Adam insisted we return to where we'd parked. He said we'd have to forget about dinner in town, and just eat at home instead. "In fact," he continued, "I want you to drive home with me. Leave your car. We'll pick it up tomorrow."

"But we're leaving for the safe house in the morning," I reminded him.

Adam swore and raked his fingers through his hair. "It doesn't matter. I'll make arrangements for Erin to pick your car up while Stowe is driving us out to the safe house."

"Okay." I nodded as we turned back.

I really wished we could still try out the new restaurant, maybe grab a takeout order at the very least, but I knew not to press the issue. Ruslan could very easily be behind the wheel of the dark mystery car with the tinted windows. Hell, he'd been spotted a couple of days earlier not far from where we were right now. And I certainly didn't want to hang around long enough for Adam to end up hurt...or worse.

My hand was still entwined with Adam's, so when he picked up the pace, I had to as well. His long strides gave me no choice, and we began to walk faster and faster. We were moving so quickly, in fact, that I almost stumbled when we ground to a stop at a red light at a cross street.

There was no traffic, though, so we stepped out onto the road.

And that was when all hell broke loose.

When we were halfway across the street, the black sedan came into view. It was somehow only yards away. The bright headlights were blinding, causing both Adam and me to freeze in the middle of the street.

Only seconds were elapsing, but each one felt more like a drawn-out minute.

Seemingly in slow motion, I screamed, "Adam, watch out."

As the words left my mouth, Adam shoved me up to the sidewalk.

I was out of danger. I was safe.

But the man I loved remained in danger. Adam was still partially on the street. And the black car was bearing down on him at a high rate of speed.

I glanced at Adam, and he shook his head at me. "Don't do anything stupid," his expression was saying.

Feeling helpless, I watched as the car approached, faster and faster. Adam drew his gun, but what would it matter? He was about to be run down.

I thought of all the choices I'd made since returning to Harbour Falls. I thought of the lies I'd told Adam in the past. Sure, I'd long since come clean, but I supposed a part of me would always feel guilty for lying so much.

So, at that very second, I knew what I had to do, what was required of me to make amends for my former selfish behavior.

I had to save Adam.

And the only way to do that was to sacrifice myself.

But, for Adam, I could be selfless.

I stepped back out onto the road, and with every ounce of strength I had, I shoved Adam Ward out of the path of the oncoming vehicle.

It was no easy task, but since I'd caught him off-guard—focused on the car heading toward him—I was successful in pushing him off-balance. Just a touch, but in the time it took for him to recover, he remained out of the path of danger.

I, unfortunately, remained right the hell in that path.

The impact came quickly, knocking me off my feet and knocking the wind out of my lungs. My left shoulder burned like a fire had been ignited in my veins. I was sure my arm was dislocated, as it seemed to sustain the brunt of the impact.

In what still felt like slow-motion, my head hit the pavement.

And that was when everything went dark.

Chapter Sixteen

W as I dead?

Maybe, as I no longer felt any pain.

In fact, I felt nothing, nothing at all. No, check that, I was experiencing a kind of floating feeling. And I could obviously hear my own thoughts. But there seemed to be nothing else.

But, then...oh, wait.

I heard Adam calling my name. It sounded as if it was from afar at first, but then the voice grew louder. Adam sounded panicked, more upset than I'd ever heard him.

I tried to reply, but I couldn't find my own voice to answer. Perhaps worse than having no voice, though, was having no sense of sight.

I tried to open my eyes to see what was going on, but nothing happened. I couldn't even feel my eyelids. I felt nothing.

And then the strangest thing occurred...

Suddenly, it was as if every sense was not only returned to me, but that each one was significantly heightened.

It all started with my hearing.

Adam's plea of, "Hang on, Maddy," was not just a whisper at my ear. It was a resonating roar in my head. An ambulance siren wailed in the distance. *So loud,* I thought.

And then a car pulled up close to where I lay, the engine idled. Someone got out, and the door slammed shut. I heard a man's voice; he asked Adam a few questions.

Wait.

I knew that voice; it belonged to Stowe. So Stowe was here. But then he was gone again. Like, in the space of a heartbeat. Speaking of which, my heart, though faint and slow, was pumping.

Not dead yet, I concluded.

Despite my sluggish heartbeats, my hearing remained acute, as did my other senses, most noticeably taste and smell.

I tasted blood in my mouth, coppery and thick. I smelled pavement and car exhaust. I tasted heartache that I might be leaving Adam. I tasted regret. But I also smelled Adam— spicy, masculine—and that soothed me.

Maybe I did have a chance. Maybe I'd make it.

I felt Adam touch me, and in my head, I breathed out, "I love you, Adam."

"I love you, Maddy," I heard him say back. "Hang in there, baby."

Maybe I *had* said my words out loud? Why else would he reply?

I choked up. Not in reality, but in my mind.

And then I gasped in horror, because my sight was suddenly returned to me. And what I saw disturbed me.

I wasn't looking up at Adam, as I should have been from my vantage point on the ground. No, I was looking *down* on the scene as Adam remained bent over my prone body.

And that could mean only one thing: I had died.

*

I wasn't dead, of course. But I was seriously injured, hallucinating as I drifted in and out of consciousness.

One thing I knew for certain, though, was that I was still lying on the street. But then I felt something being slipped beneath me, a hard slab, a stretcher, no doubt. I was shifted and secured, and then lifted up and into an ambulance to be transported to the hospital.

Adam was at my side as two paramedics spoke in low voices as they worked on me. I felt Adam's hand wrap around mine, warm and comforting. He asked one of the paramedics how I was doing.

"She has a fairly serious head injury, sir," one paramedic replied.

"And a fractured shoulder,' the other paramedic said, "numerous cuts and abrasions, too. But it's the head injury that we're most concerned with."

That doesn't sound good, I thought as I drifted back to a state of unconsciousness.

I awoke some time later, groggy and in pain. Although my lids felt thick and heavy, I was able to open my eyes.

I was in a hospital room, and Adam was in a chair next to my bed.

I shifted, but the pain was so bad I couldn't help but cry out.

Adam was up and leaning over me in an instant. "Maddy, Maddy, don't move, okay?"

"Everything hurts so much," I whimpered.

Adam touched my cheek lightly, and I said, "Well, that doesn't hurt."

"I know you're in pain, Maddy," Adam replied. "But the doctors won't give you any pain meds until they get your CT scan results back. They need to make certain there's no swelling of the brain."

I tried to nod, but even that action caused discomfort.

"You should rest," Adam said softly.

But I had to know something first. "Who hit me? Was it Ruslan? He was the person driving the car with the tinted windows, wasn't he?"

"Yes, Maddy, it was Ruslan who hit you." Adam lowered his voice and added, "But you don't have to worry about him anymore. None of us do."

I searched Adam's eyes. "He's dead?" I whispered.

Adam nodded slowly.

"Did you..."

"No," he said, eliciting from me a breath I hadn't realized I was holding.

I was glad Adam had not killed Ruslan.

I remembered hearing Stowe's voice at the scene, so I ventured, "So, Stowe..."

Even though I trailed off, leaving my question unfinished, Adam knew what I was asking. And he replied, "Yes, Maddy. Stowe took care of Ruslan."

"What happened?"

I didn't want blow-by-blow details, but I was curious as to how everything had gone down.

Adam blew out a breath. "I was with you in the ambulance, so this is just what I've been told thus far." He paused, shooting me a worried look.

"Go on," I said.

"Ruslan wrecked a few streets away after he ran you down. I thought I heard a crash—that's what I told Stowe when he stopped—but I wasn't sure exactly where the accident had occurred. I was too worried about you at that point. I didn't care about fucking Ruslan and his whereabouts." Adam sighed. "Didn't matter, though... Stowe found him."

Adam didn't have to say anything more.

Stowe had found and killed our tormentor. And being the consummate professional that he was, I was sure Stowe had disposed of all the evidence. Surely, once Stowe was finished, it would be as if Ruslan had never existed.

"So, it's all over, then?" I asked Adam.

"Yeah, Maddy, it's over. We're safe now."

I couldn't help it; I began to cry. The weight lifting from my shoulders felt enormous. It seemed that at no time in my relationship with Adam had I ever felt truly safe. There was always something going on—always. Whether it was my fearing that Adam himself might turn out to be danger-ous—like during the Harbour Falls Mystery—or the many other dangers I'd faced, there was always something to be dealt with. And true, I'd craved that brand of danger for so long. But now that I'd been touched by it—coming close to death, even—I was ready for more tranquil times.

Adam gathered me to him as best as he could without hurting me. "Maddy, Maddy...don't cry, sweetheart."

I tried to rein in my tears, but I needed to know one more thing. "Are all the secret and dangerous jobs done, Adam?" I choked out. "Can you promise me you'll just work with boring, safe clients from now on?"

Adam leaned back. "Boring and safe?" He chuckled. "Now where would the fun be in that?"

He was teasing, trying to get me to laugh, but I needed his word. "It's not funny, Adam. Please, promise me. I'm serious."

Adam's eyes were so blue, so clear. The burden had been lifted from him as well. "I promise, Maddy," he quietly vowed. "No more projects like Wickingham Way."

"Thank you," I whispered, relieved.

With relief came tiredness. I was suddenly very sleepy. I knew trouble of some sort would probably always follow

Adam. He was just too powerful of a man to live a life completely free from danger. But the prospect of just a tiny bit of danger I could live with. I expected it might even help keep things fresh and interesting.

So, yeah, I concluded life with Adam would never be boring. But at least with his promise, being around him would never again turn out to be potentially deadly.

Chapter Seventeen

M y CT scans came back normal, and I was released from the hospital a few days later.

I had been very lucky, the doctors informed me. I was covered in bruises and had to wear a sling for my injured shoulder, but otherwise I was fine and I'd heal completely.

Adam picked me up at the hospital the afternoon I was released and drove me back to my Harbour Falls rental. He was unusually quiet, and when I asked him why, he gave me no good explanation.

A quiet Adam usually meant he was up to something. And sure enough, when I walked into the house I was greeted with a raucous chorus of, "Surprise!"

"Maddy, welcome home," my dad said when things quieted down. He was smiling as he stood by the living room doorway.

"Oh my goodness," I breathed out.

I was frozen in the entry area, truly surprised by our gathered friends and family.

Adam remained close behind me, his hand protectively situated at the small of my back. "Surprise party," he whispered as he leaned in. "In case you haven't figured it out," he added with a chuckle.

My father had tears in his eyes as he stepped forward and gave me a careful half-hug. Nate and Helena were behind my dad, smiling.

"You're back from the safe house," I said to our friends when my dad stepped off to the side. "This is great!"

Helena rushed to me and hugged me as carefully as my father had. Everyone was being so cautious with me, I feel like I was made of glass. But I appreciated their concern. It was cute, especially Adam's frown when Helena paid no heeds to his protests and insisted on being the one to help me to the living room sofa.

"Who else is here?" I asked as I sank down onto the floral-patterned cushions.

"Stowe and Erin are in the kitchen, and Max is supposed to stop by later," Helena replied.

"How is Max?" I asked.

"He's great, just about fully healed."

Glancing around, I asked, "So, Stowe and Erin are in the...kitchen?"

I wasn't sure if I'd heard Helena correctly before, but I supposed I had since she confirmed, "Yep, in the kitchen. They've been preparing food all morning."

"You're kidding." I arched an eyebrow.

It was hard to imagine two assassins slaving away in the kitchen.

I started to laugh, and Helena said, "I know, right?"

We quieted, though, when Stowe, at that exact second, walked into the living room.

Stowe was dutifully carrying trays of fried chicken and baked beans, while Erin trailed behind. Her expression was nothing short of serious as she cradled various cold salads in her arms.

Once they noticed me on the sofa, and after setting the trays down on a long buffet table under the window, Stowe and Erin each took turns giving me hugs and welcoming me home.

"You don't have to do that," I said to Erin when she went back over to the table and began to prepare me a plate of food.

"Maddy, hush." Erin waved her free hand my way. "This may be the only time I ever wait on you like this, so enjoy it."

Probably true, since Erin didn't strike me as the hostess type. But I had to say she and Stowe seemed to be reveling in the host and hostess roles today.

I gladly accepted the plate, which was overflowing with food, when Erin passed it to Stowe, who then handed it to me.

"There's cake, too, Maddy," Stowe said as he turned back toward the kitchen. "I'll go grab it now. Erin did most of the work, but I did help with the frosting."

Erin laughed and then tried to cover it up with a cough when Stowe appeared miffed.

Oh goodness. I smiled at the thought of assassin-Stowe frosting a cake.

Apparently done with waitressing duties, Erin sat down next to me on the sofa. Helena, seated at my other side, nodded to her.

I glanced up at Adam, who was leaning against the doorjamb, taking it all in. He smiled, and mouthed, "Welcome home."

I knew Adam had a hand in the surprise party, so I mouthed back, "Thank you."

My dad and Nate, who'd just finished loading up their own plates with piles of food, gestured for Adam to follow them into the dining room as they walked past him. Adam shot me a final smile, then turned away and left with Dad and Nate.

Two seconds later, Stowe returned from the kitchen carrying the cake he'd help frost. After plopping it down on the coffee table—there was no more room on the buffet—Stowe excused himself and left to join the guys in the dining room.

"Guess they've had enough of us," I joked, motioning toward the departing Stowe with my uninjured arm.

"Good," Helena said as she bit into a piece of chicken. "More time for girl talk," she added between more bites.

After all I'd been through, some lighthearted girl talk sounded good to me.

I began to cut a piece of the haphazardly frosted cake Stowe had placed on the table. But when I had a little trouble, Erin once again pitched in.

"Maddy," she said as she cut a piece of cake and plated it. "You should have seen Stowe helping me prepare all of this. Oh my God, it was comical, especially when it was time to frost the cake."

Despite the less-than-stellar frosting job, Helena eyed the piece of cake Erin had cut as she set it down in front of me.

"Oh my God, chocolate-on-chocolate," Helena gushed. "I absolutely have to have some."

"Someone sure is hungry," I teased as Helena leaned over and cut a very large piece of cake for herself.

Helena licked at the chocolate frosting she'd gotten on her fingers. "I'm eating for two, Miss Maddy. Need I remind you?"

"Good point," I replied.

Erin's eyebrows rose as she directed her attention to Helena. "What? You're pregnant?"

I'd forgotten that Erin hadn't yet been told the good news. The day she'd walked in on us in the kitchen, after Helena had shared her happy news with me, the subject had been changed. And Helena wasn't showing much at all, so her condition wasn't blatantly obvious.

"Yep, I'm knocked up," Helena confirmed, smiling. "Almost three months."

I could tell it thrilled Helena to say those words. Adam had told me in confidence that Helena and Nate had tried for years to have children, but to no avail. They'd given up long ago, thinking it just wasn't meant to be. And now... Well, I knew this baby meant the world to both of them.

"You look fantastic," Erin said. "Any morning sickness?"

"A little at first, but, at the time, I thought I was just under the weather."

I thought back to the day Helena had accompanied me to Willow Point, to when her stepfather had held us hostage in the old asylum basement. "Oh God, Helena, you were pregnant *then*?"

She knew I was referring to Willow Point, and she nodded solemnly. "I was, but I didn't know until a week or so later."

I shuddered, thinking of how close to harm we'd both come. And an unborn baby had been at risk as well. "Thank God Stowe got there when he did," I said.

Helena quietly agreed.

I wasn't sure if Erin knew all the details of the Willow Point incident, but when I asked her if she did, she said Stowe had filled her in on everything that had happened.

"That's right," I said. "Stowe was working with you even then, right?"

"He was." Erin sighed. "And Maddy, I have to apologize again. I still feel bad for keeping so many things from Adam back then."

I assured her that Adam had long ago forgiven her. Besides, Agent Lenehan had only been complying with government orders. It wasn't like she had left Adam out of the loop for kicks.

"Everything worked out all right, anyway," I added.

"Yeah," Helena chimed in, "and you ended up with Stowe. How crazy is that?"

Erin nodded, her cheeks reddening a touch.

Helena must have noticed. She slyly stated, "Speaking of Stowe... You never did tell us what he's into. You know, like sexually."

Erin's face grew as red as the highlights in her hair.

"Helena!" I kicked my friend's foot. "That's none of our business."

"We talked about it before," Helena protested.

"It's okay," Erin interjected. "I'm not going to go into specific details or anything, but I will say Stowe is very, uh, adventurous."

"Adventurous in what way? Role playing, bondage?"

My eyes widened as I turned to Helena, shocked at her forwardness. Not to mention the fact she'd even thrown out those terms.

Role playing? Bondage?

"Something you'd like to share?" I asked Helena. "Does Nate have a secret kinky side?"

Helena shook her head and sighed wistfully. "No, not really, though I sometimes wish he did. I do read a lot, you know, so I'm well-aware of those things. And I have to say some of them sound fun."

"They are," Erin murmured dreamily.

Helena and I both turned to Erin, wide-eyed and ready to hear the dirt.

But Erin never had a chance to divulge Stowe's kinky proclivities. Nate yelled from the dining room for Helena and the whole conversation was interrupted.

"I swear, that man," Helena griped as she stood. "He has the worst timing."

"We'll continue this when you get back," Erin promised.

However, once Helena was out of the room, my discussion with Erin turned to something more serious—the Wickingham Way project.

"So, it's really all over," I quietly inquired. "Ruslan is definitely dead."

"He's definitely dead, Maddy," Erin assured me.

"Since everything's over," I continued, "I'm guessing you and Stowe will be leaving Harbour Falls soon."

Erin sighed. "Yeah, pretty soon."

I'd grown to like Agent Lenehan, and it saddened me to think she was leaving so soon. Hell, I'd even miss Stowe Hannigan. After all, he'd been a friend all along, even when I hadn't thought so.

"Where will you and Stowe live?" I asked.

"Boston."

That made perfect sense. Erin lived in Boston already, and now that Stowe was no longer part of the defunct criminal organization in Florida, he had no real home.

Since Adam's sister's wedding was coming up in another month, I threw out, "Maybe Adam and I can visit you and Stowe when we come down for Trina and Walker's wedding in May."

"That'd be nice," Erin replied, smiling.

At that point, Helena returned, as did the guys. Sadly, our kinky sex talk had to be tabled for another day. But maybe that was for the best, as Erin didn't seem entirely comfortable divulging Stowe's kinky side. And she'd been interrupted twice, so maybe her telling us the details wasn't meant to be. I made a decision to squelch my curiosity. Hell, I guessed I was finally learning to accept that I didn't need to know everything about everyone. What a change for me from the autumn.

As the day wore into evening, everyone sat around, talking and laughing. It was good to have our friends gathered. Max showed up at seven, apologizing for having taken so long to arrive on the mainland.

"Sorry, I got tied up with those renovations," I overheard him say to Adam.

The lighthouse, I thought.

So much was changing. Renovations on the island, the Wickingham Way project coming to a close, Stowe and Erin leaving town, and last but not least, Helena and Nate expecting their first child.

And then there was me and Adam…

I knew we'd be heading back over to Fade Island soon, as the lease was up on the Victorian in two weeks. Mrs. Heider would be returning from Florida and reclaiming her property.

But that was fine with me. I was ready to return to the island, ready to move forward with Adam. After all, he still hadn't proposed.

But I had a strong feeling that he was going to ask me to marry him very, very soon.

Chapter Eighteen

Adam and I returned to Fade Island the very next week.

I was thrilled to be back, thrilled to leave behind the house I'd been renting in Harbour Falls. I originally leased Mrs. Heider's Victorian before breaking up with Adam. When I left the island in January, it was under the guise of leaving the man I loved. On a dark winter evening, I'd found Adam down in the wine cellar and told him I needed time apart. How far from the truth those words had been.

I vowed to never say them again.

It seemed so far away now—that phony breakup—but it had occurred only three months earlier. Not only had a lot changed in my relationship with Adam—we were more solid than ever these days—but I soon discovered things had changed on the island as well.

First, the owners of the storefronts along Main Street had returned to Fade Island. The morning Adam and I returned, we'd driven up from the dock to find many of the store proprietors out on the sidewalks, washing down windows and re-hanging signage that had been taken down for the off season. Early preparations for the upcoming tourist season were well underway.

"I can't believe winter's finally over," I had said to Adam as we'd passed the shops.

He'd put his hand on my knee, and murmured, "Well, it is, Maddy. And wait until you see how beautiful the island is this time of year."

Adam was not kidding. Winter was nothing but a distant memory on Fade Island. As we'd driven along the coast-line, I took note of how spring certainly was in full bloom. If I'd thought Mrs. Heider's flower beds were impressive, Id been sadly mistaken. Tulips of every tone and color, as well as varying shades of yellow daffodils, dotted the island landscape.

All of that occurred yesterday, but I was still in awe of the beautiful springtime island displays today. In fact, I was standing out in front of my cottage, admiring some of that floral beauty right in my own front yard.

"Pretty," I said to no one in particular as I scanned the grassy expanse that was dotted with vividly colored daffo-dils, crocuses, and tulips.

I would have been talking to Adam about the loveli-ness of the island, had he been with me. But today I was on my own. Adam was over on the mainland, working at his Harbour Falls office until evening.

As I lingered on the walkway, my eyes were drawn to the window boxes. I'd planted chrysanthemums in the box closest to the front door back in the fall. Sadly, though the plants were still in the box, the once-white blooms had seen better days.

I sighed, recalling how Max had brought two pot-ted flowers to me as a peace offering after he'd caught me trespassing on Adam's property. He had felt bad that he'd scared me to the point of fainting that fateful night. I smiled now, thinking of how Max slipped up the morning he brought the flowers. He confessed that it was Adam who'd suggested the white mums, something I'd mentioned to

Ami I was interested in purchasing. Seemed Mr. Ward had been attentive and observant right from the start.

I wished the reminders of my early days with Adam could remain forever, but the blossoms had long since shriveled and dried up. I moved over to the window boxes and dug out what was left of the mums. Once my task was completed, I swiped my hands on my jeans to brush off the soil on my fingers.

"Well, what next?" I mused as I glanced around.

I'd traveled down to the cottage to retrieve the last few belongings I'd left there. I was more or less moved in with Adam, living with him at the large estate a mile north from where I currently stood. Adam and Max had moved the last of my big stuff the evening before. Now I was here just to grab some books I'd left on the shelves inside. Adam warned me not to overdo it, though, as I was still recovering from being hit by the car driven by Ruslan. My shoulder remained in a sling and would for another month.

Cognizant of Adam's request that I not push myself and reinjure my shoulder, I was careful when I went inside and packed up the last of my books. I took the boxes out and loaded them into the silver Navigator I drove when on the island.

Just as I was placing the last box in the SUV, Max drove by. I waved, and he quickly pulled his dark green Hummer into the driveway, parking it behind my Navigator.

Max rolled down the window and called out, "Hey, Maddy, how's it going today? Do you need any help with anything?"

I looked around. All the boxes were secured in the vehicle, so I replied, "No, I don't think so. I'm actually just about ready to go."

Max nodded, and then I asked, "Hey, where are you headed?"

I was kind of bored, and Adam wouldn't be back on the island for a few more hours. I had time to kill.

"Down to the lighthouse," Max replied. "Work is just about finished up down there. But there are a few things I need to check on before the guys leave today."

Adam had finally fessed up that he was indeed having the lighthouse renovated, just as I'd suspected. I'd yet to see the refurbished structure, though, so I asked Max, "Do you mind if I go down there with you?"

He shrugged. "If you want to, it's fine with me."

Since there were people I didn't know on the island, getting things ready for summer, I locked the Nav. Then, with Max's help, I hopped up into the passenger seat of his Hummer.

And we were off.

Max parked at the lower end of Main Street. He cut the engine and helped me down from his vehicle. He took extra care when I shifted funny and winced at the resulting sharp pain in my injured shoulder.

"You all right?" he asked as I stepped down.

"Yeah, I think so."

The narrow, gravel pathway that trailed toward the steep set of steps cut into the high cliffs was directly to my right. Max and I stepped onto the trail and headed toward the steps.

I glanced over at him as we walked. Adam had told me Max was completely healed from his gunshot wound. Still, I felt compelled to ask, "How are you feeling?"

Max smiled gently. "Good, Maddy. What about you?" He nodded his chin to my shoulder. "Shoulder healing up okay?"

I nodded. "Yeah, it's healing. Of course, it still hurts when I move certain ways, but the doctors say that's to be expected. Overall, it's coming along nicely."

Max said he was happy I'd not suffered any worse damage, and then we dropped the subject. It seemed neither of us cared to dwell on how we'd been injured by Ruslan and his cohorts.

The close of the subject came at the perfect time too, just as we reached the end of the trail.

It was a clear day—blue skies, sunny—so the lighthouse at the end of the strip of land below was fully visible. And it looked amazing!

The stark white structure had always loomed in the background of the landscape of oil-black rocks that dotted the thin strip of land leading out into the sea. But with the new paint job the lighthouse stood proudly, taller and whiter and brighter than ever.

I turned to Max, and asked, "Can we go down?"

"Sure. I need to talk to the workers, anyway." He jerked his chin in the direction of where a few men were milling around the lighthouse.

I clapped my hands excitedly, and Max added, "Just stay close to me, Maddy. We cleared out a nice path—wider than before—but it can still be a treacherous trek. Adam would kill me if you slipped and got hurt."

Max sounded truly worried. I found it somewhat comical that this huge man who'd *killed* people feared Adam Ward. But Adam could be intimidating, no doubt. Any man with that much authority and power was bound to be feared. It thrilled me in a way, because Adam was all mine. I'd captured the heart of a powerful man.

Heeding Max's request, I was mindful of my steps as we made our way down to the lighthouse. I didn't want to end up hurt and have Max feel responsible, so I stayed close to him, all the way until we reached the base of the lighthouse. There, the workers spotted Max and greeted him with a barrage of questions.

I stepped back a few feet to give everyone some space to talk. But when Max was done speaking to the workers, he headed back over to where I stood.

"Sorry about that," he said.

I waved my hand. "Oh, don't worry about it."

I glanced around at all the improvements to the area around the lighthouse. The sandy trail leading up to the structure had been widened, and flowers had been planted in between the rocks on either side of the trail, giving the lighthouse a much more welcoming feel than before.

I wondered how things looked inside the structure. Surely the lighthouse was no longer dark, cold, and musty, like the last time I'd been in it.

"So, what all is Adam having done down here?" I asked, anxious to veer my thoughts away from the night I'd been held captive in the structure before me.

Max listed off many of the improvements that had been made: fresh coats of paint inside and out, a change in the interior lighting, better access to the lantern room, and various aesthetic touches, like the flowers.

"And," Max said as he finished his spiel. "Adam wants the beacon working again."

"Oh, wow, how cool." I tilted back my head and stared up at the top of the lighthouse.

Fade Island would once again have a working lighthouse.

I loved all of the improvements Adam had ordered, and like I'd told my guy, this place held only good memories for me. Well, not completely. But now that the lighthouse looked so different, I vowed to myself that I would no longer allow the events that had occurred with Jennifer and Ami to overshadow my good memories. Good memories, like the one I had of Adam bringing me down to the lighthouse for the first time...or the one of Adam trying to kiss me up in the lantern room.

I was about to ask if we could go inside, but just then Max got a text. "I'm afraid I have to take you back to the cottage, Maddy," he said as he read his message. "I have some other things to attend to right now."

"I understand," I told him. "I should probably get back, too."

We headed back up to Max's Hummer, and after he dropped me off at the cottage, I got in my own SUV and drove up to Adam's estate. On the way, I kept thinking of how much I loved Adam. Spending time down at the lighthouse had reminded me of how much he turned me on, even back then, even when I wasn't sure at all if Adam could be trusted.

Adam and I hadn't done much physically since I'd gotten hurt, and I missed that connection. I knew Adam didn't want to reinjure my shoulder. That was why he was being so extra cautious. But I needed to reconnect with him. The lighthouse had reminded me of all the hot feelings we were keeping at bay.

I made a decision, just as I turned into the driveway of Adam's compound. I was going to unleash all those pent-up feelings tonight. Hell, my shoulder felt good enough for *that* kind of physical activity.

But first, I needed to prepare. And I needed a plan—a plan to seduce Adam.

After I was parked, I raced into the house.

First, I checked to make sure Adam wasn't home yet.

All was quiet, the coast was clear.

I hurried upstairs, where I showered and dressed in the sexiest lingerie I could find—black bra, matching panties, black stockings, and garters. Adam wasn't going to know what hit him when he walked through the bedroom door.

Since I expected Adam to arrive at any time, I hastily propped up some pillows on the massive bed in the master bedroom and leaned back against them. I'd slipped the sling off for the night, as it was messing with the whole sexy vibe.

After a few moments, I heard the front door opening and closing.

Adam was home.

When I heard him ascending the stairs, I bent my leg at the knee and fluffed out my hair.

There, ready... My seduction was in place.

When Adam walked into the bedroom, the look on his handsome face was priceless. He sure hadn't expected to find me laid out before him like a present just waiting to be unwrapped.

"See anything you like?" I asked when he hesitated in the doorway, his eyes raking hungrily over my body.

A sly smile tugged at the corner of his mouth. "Maddy, Maddy," he tsked. "You really think you're up for this?"

"I think the more appropriate question, Mr. Ward, is this: are you up for this?" I lifted an eyebrow.

Adam chuckled and undid his tie. He tossed the silk material aside and strode over to the bed. His eyes, as he approached, seared me with intensity.

Adam shrugged off his suit jacket, but when he started to unbutton his dress shirt, I stopped him. "Leave it," I said in a low voice.

I actually wanted Adam to take me as he was, dressed in a dark business suit. I wanted to be his reward at the end of a long day. I wanted Adam in control, as he was in every aspect of his business life. And the sexy Mr. Ward clothed—while I was not—would give me what I longed for: the feeling of being taken by this powerful man.

Adam, always so in tune with my needs, caught on immediately to exactly what I wanted. With a sexy smirk, he slipped his suit jacket back on. "Is this what you want, Madeleine? Me completely dressed?"

I nodded. "Uh-huh."

Adam snatched up my feet and slowly slid me to the edge of the bed. Running his hands up and down my stockinged legs, his warmth heating the cool silk, he rasped, "I really like these."

Before I had a chance to respond, Adam climbed up over my body. He straddled my chest as he unzipped his pants. Fueled with desire, I reached into his boxer briefs and wrapped my hand around him. With a harsh intake of breath, Adam reached down and freed himself from the confines of material.

With no hesitation, I took him in my mouth, hungry for every inch.

Adam placed his hand behind my head, propping me up to accept his measured thrusts more adeptly. When I increased the pace on my own, he moaned out a curse. But then, he pulled back.

"Adam," I whimpered. "Please, don't stop."

His mouth descended to mine. "I have no intention of stopping, Maddy," he said between hot, wet kisses, "I want to be inside you so fucking much right now."

With his pants still on but undone, he settled between my legs. His hot shaft pressed up against my soaked panties. I reached down to undo one of the garters, but Adam stilled my hand. "No, like this," he said.

Adam pushed my panties aside and slowly entered me, stretching and filling. I threw back my head and arched my neck. We made slow, careful love until we both found release.

"God," I breathed out, once I was able to recover my voice. "That was—"

"Amazing," Adam finished for me.

It seemed fitting, Adam completing my sentences. After all, he'd been completing me in so many other ways for a long while now.

Chapter Nineteen

When Adam returned from work the next evening, I ran right into him in the entry hall.

After making sure I was all right, he suggested we take a little drive. I knew immediately Adam was up to something, something good.

"And exactly where will we be going?" I asked, knowing there were only a limited number of possibilities here on the small island, especially since the sun was setting.

Adam placed his hands on my shoulders and leaned down to whisper in my ear, "It's a surprise, Madeleine. But do wear something nice. I have a few business things to wrap up, but let's say we meet back here in the entry hall in"—Adam glanced at his watch—"thirty minutes?"

"Okay," I agreed.

I considered asking for more detail on where we were going, but before I could question Adam any further, he was halfway down the hall, heading toward his newly remodeled study.

"Huh," I mused out loud.

Thirty minutes wasn't long, so I hurried upstairs to get ready for our mystery date. If Adam wanted me dressed up tonight, then that's what he was going to get.

I showered in the en suite bathroom, dried off in the master bedroom. Most all of my clothes now occupied one entire side of Adam's walk-in closet, so I tightened the towel around my body and stepped into the massive space. After a short deliberation, I chose a slinky black evening gown. There was a slit up one side of the gown and a plunging neckline, two little details I knew Adam loved in these kinds of dresses.

Perfect.

Adam remained downstairs while I readied for our date. I assumed he was finishing his business and getting ready in one of the many bedrooms and bathrooms available to him on the first floor. Adam rarely used any of those facilities—they were mostly for guests—but since I was monopolizing the master bedroom and bath, it made sense that he'd clean up and dress downstairs for our date.

Sure enough, when I started down the long, spiral staircase, Adam emerged from one of the hallways, looking stunning. I stopped in my tracks, teetering slightly in my heels.

"Oh my," I muttered.

Adam glanced up at me and smiled, making him all the more alluring. Not that he needed anything more to add to his appeal. Dressed in a sleek black tux, as he was tonight, Adam was nothing short of exquisite.

I supposed I looked okay myself. Adam eyed me appreciably, and I viewed that response as a positive sign.

I felt even more confident, though, when I reached the base of the stairs and Adam purred, "You are a gorgeous woman, Madeleine Fitch. Don't ever think any differently."

I blushed as he offered me his hand. "Thank you, Mr. Ward," I murmured. "You look pretty damn good yourself."

Adam chuckled and thanked me. "Ready?" he asked.

"Still not giving up the goods on where we're going?"

His blue eyes sparkled. "No way, baby. No way."

*

When I was settled in the Range Rover, Adam reached over from the driver's seat and blindfolded me.

"Is this really necessary?" I asked as he straightened the black, silky-feeling material over my eyes.

"Yes, it is, Maddy," I was told.

I huffed, but purely in fun. I actually liked the excitement of not knowing where we were heading. Oh, sure, I had an idea we were going down to the lighthouse. It was the only place that made sense, as Adam had yet to personally show me the renovations he'd had done. But I had no idea why such secrecy was required.

Adam was quiet as we drove, but he turned the car stereo on to fill the silence. A song about *feeling something in the air tonight* poured through the speakers, reminding me of my first trip over to the island.

That had happened over seven months ago, and so much had changed since then. I found it amazing how one decision could alter the course of so many lives. My decision to investigate the Harbour Falls Mystery had led to *so* many changes. Some of those changes had turned out to be bad—like losing Jimmy. But (thankfully) many good things, as well, had come from investigating the mystery—the best thing being that I had reconnected with the man currently at my side. My high school crush, the love of my life: Adam Ward.

"What are you thinking about, Maddy?" Adam asked when I blew out a breath.

Adam turned down the stereo, and I said, "Oh, I don't know. Mostly, I was thinking about us."

Adam reached over and squeezed my hand. "What about us?"

I sighed. "Lots of stuff... But all that really matters is that in the end we reconnected with each other."

"That we did," Adam murmured as the Range Rover rolled to a stop.

Before I knew what was happening, Adam's hot mouth descended upon mine. The blindfold had allowed him to catch me off guard, and I liked being able to *feel* Adam without seeing him. It made his every touch more intense, particularly when he slid one hand into the plunging neckline of my dress.

I gasped as his fingers expertly plied a nipple. "No bra," he rasped against my mouth.

"No bra," I confirmed with a whispery little moan.

"Do you want me to stop?" Adam asked. "We don't have to do this here."

"I want to do this here," I insisted, my breaths growing more and more ragged.

Adam began to undo my blindfold, but my hand covered his. "Leave it," I whispered.

I couldn't see Adam, but I sensed he was smiling. He wanted that blindfold left on as much as I did.

Slowly, Adam's hand slid under the slit in my dress. When he found I'd nixed not only a bra but underwear as well, he *tsk*ed. "Oh, Madeleine, you are very naughty."

With the blindfold on, everything was dark for me. Although I assumed full darkness had fallen outside. I hoped so, since I didn't have any clue as to where we were parked.

Hopefully not in the middle of Main Street for all to see, I thought.

Even though I was pretty certain Adam had parked in a discreet location, the idea that he might not have turned me on even further. I was feeling wild tonight, wet and wanton. Blindfolded as I was, I wanted Adam to take me in a raw, primal way. Like he had before I'd been injured.

Thankfully, I got what I wanted.

I heard Adam unzip his pants, right before he pulled me on to his lap. He adjusted all the silky material of my gown until it was bunched up around my hips. My bare center pressed to Adam's hard length, but he made no move to enter me, even though he had to feel me throbbing against him.

"Adam," I begged, but he silenced me with his mouth, opening my lips to accept his tongue.

Without breaking the kiss, he undid the clasp behind my neck that held the top of the dress in place. The material fell away, exposing my breasts to Adam. He cupped the heavy flesh, kneading and plying. And then, without warning, he shifted and plunged into me.

I yelped, caught unexpected, still blindfolded. Like this, I was a slave to sensation. My breasts bounced as Adam slid me up and down his length. His mouth descended to one nipple...then the other...and I threw my head back in ecstasy as he worshipped my breasts. Adam held me in his grasp, moving with me and within me as I writhed on his lap.

When he raised his head from my chest, he growled, "Tell me you're mine."

He thrust up into me, hard, three times...four times... five.

"I'm yours, I'm yours," I cried out as we came, my walls spasming around his pulsing cock.

I was overwhelmed, and tears spilled from my eyes. I wasn't sad, I'd just never felt this incredibly happy.

Adam removed the blindfold and dabbed at my eyes with the material. His indigo blues met my gaze. "Hey, I'm yours just as much as you're mine," he said softly. "You know this, right?"

I nodded. "I know, Adam. I know."

And I did. We belonged to no others, only to ourselves.

Adam helped me re-clasp and straighten all the material of my gown. He did up his pants while I checked my face in the mirror. Surprisingly, my make-up had held up quite well.

Now that the blindfold was off, I took in my surroundings. It was very dark out, the sky a velvety black. Adam had parked in a secluded spot, high above the cliffs overlooking the lighthouse.

What I didn't notice though, until we got out of the SUV, was that someone had strung yards and yards of clear lights along the path leading to the steps cut into the cliff.

"Ooh, this is so pretty," I said to Adam as we walked, the path lit up and glowing before us.

Adam smiled, and taking my hand, he led us to the edge of the cliff, to where the steps descended to the lighthouse.

"Oh, Adam," I exclaimed.

The scene below was beautiful. The clear lights extended all the way down the steps and then continued along the widened path that led to the lighthouse.

The lighthouse itself, it was a sight to behold.

Not only was the structure a bright white tower in the distance—even in the darkness—but the beacon at the top glowed brightly as it rotated round and round. And every time the bright light made a pass in the direction of the cliffs, a huge sign that had been placed in the curve of cliff rock to our left was illuminated.

The sign, written in Adam's concise script, read: "Maddy, please say yes."

I looked up at Adam and coyly asked, "Say yes to what, Adam?"

This stunning man who I always found myself looking up to lowered himself to one bended knee and presented me with the black velvet box I'd seen in the jewelry store. He popped the lid up, and a platinum ring with an emerald-cut diamond shimmered in the moonlight.

In a low voice, Adam gazed up at me and quietly murmured, "Marry me, Madeleine Fitch."

Chapter Twenty

"Yes," I said. "Yes, yes, of course I'll marry you." I bounced on my toes and threw my arms around Adam as he stood to his full height.

I kissed that man like there'd be no tomorrow. But there would be a tomorrow, and I'd be an engaged woman when it dawned.

I said this to Adam, and he replied, "No waiting until tomorrow, Maddy. Let's make it official, right here, right now." He slipped the dazzling ring onto my finger and said, "*Now* you're officially engaged."

"To you," I whispered.

"To me," Adam replied as he leaned down to kiss me once more, this time more deeply, more soulfully.

"I love you," he said when our lips slowed to a stop.

I tilted my head back slightly and looked up into his eyes. "I love you too, Adam. And I can't wait to become Mrs. Madeleine Ward."

Adam quirked an eyebrow. "So, you'll be taking my name, then?"

He appeared very pleased to hear my admission. I knew Adam had an old-fashioned streak, and things such as these were important to him.

"I've given it a lot of thought," I said. "And I've decided I'd be honored to share your name."

"What about your books?" Adam queried. "You use your real name. All your readers know you as Madeleine Fitch. Nobody will know who Madeleine Ward is."

"I've considered that," I replied, thoughtful about it even now. "I don't want to *not* use your name, though, so I've decided to hyphenate our last names for my novels."

Adam loved the idea and showed me how much when our lips met once more.

Eventually, after a bit more making out, Adam suggested we start down to the lighthouse. "There's more to this surprise than just a proposal up here on the ledge."

"The proposal would be enough," I said. "Honestly."

And it would have been, but I knew Adam had much more planned for our evening. I just didn't know what.

"Are you hungry?" he asked as we carefully negotiated our way down the steep set of steps cut into the face of the cliffs.

"Actually"—I held tightly to Adam's arm as I spoke—"I am."

"Good. Dinner is all set up in the lighthouse."

"Aw, the lighthouse," I said. "I knew it figured in to your plans tonight."

"Smart girl," Adam retorted.

When I'd ventured down to the lighthouse with Max, I'd viewed the exterior only. But now I'd have the chance to check out all the improvements Adam had had made to the interior.

When I stepped inside, I was in complete awe.

The lighthouse was beautiful inside. What had once been dim and musty was now bright and airy. The interior had been painted a soft white. And there was all new lighting, giving off a warm, welcoming glow.

I wasn't sure who Adam had employed to get things ready for this evening—the workers, Max, maybe even Erin—but what they'd accomplished was impressive. A small, round table was set up in the center of the lighthouse, with two chairs placed on either side. Vases of various heights were filled with fresh-cut flowers. They lined the floor and iron staircase. Candles adorned the table, as well as a bottle of chilled champagne, crystal flutes, and two china plates topped with silver-domed covers.

Adam stepped over to the table and offered his hand. I placed my hand in his, and he led me to one of the chairs.

When Adam pulled the chair out for me, I took a seat. "Thank you," I murmured.

Adam lifted the cover on my plate and presented me with a feast: baked stuffed lobster, haricots vert, wild rice, and a cup of drawn butter. "Mmm, everything looks delicious," I murmured.

All the food was still warm, and I had to ask, "Who set this up, Adam? He or she must have just finished. How did I not see anyone leaving?"

Adam sat down and lifted his own plate cover. "I have my ways, Madeleine, I have my ways," was all he would say.

I left it at that. I'd long since learned I didn't need to know everything. Some secrets were best kept.

Adam and I ate and talked, enjoying our candlelit dinner.

"The lobster is amazing," I declared at one point.

Adam poured us each a glass of champagne. "Try this with it. I think you'll find it's an excellent complement to this particular dish."

I took a tentative sip and had to agree with Adam's assessment. He certainly knew his fine vintages.

When Adam and I were just about finished with our meals, talk turned to our relationship...and the many twists and turns it had taken.

"What were you thinking the first time I brought you down here to the lighthouse?" Adam asked as he leaned back in his chair.

I took a small sip of champagne as I thought back to that dreary fall afternoon when Adam had showed up at the café. The evening prior I'd been caught trespassing on his property. When I'd ended up in Adam's living room, we'd sparred verbally, but we'd also flirted outrageously. In some ways, that night, we rekindled an attraction that had sparked in high school. So when he showed up at the café the next day and asked me to accompany him for a stroll, I'd accepted.

I'd had no idea at the time where we were heading, but the lighthouse was where we'd ended up.

"I was nervous that evening," I admitted as I set my glass on the table. "I wasn't sure what game you were playing."

Adam leaned forward, his curiosity seemingly piqued. "Can you elaborate?"

"Well," I began, "first off, I didn't know how much you knew about why I was on the island."

"I knew everything, Maddy."

"Yeah, I kind of suspected as much when you told me I should consider writing about the mystery right in front of me." I could laugh about it all now, and I did just that.

"Ah, yes." Adam's blue eyes sparkled as he smiled. "My first attempt to get you to come clean. An attempt that had no effect, I might add."

"It did, though," I insisted. "I wanted to tell you what I was up to as soon as you asked."

"So why didn't you?" Adam asked softly.

I looked down at my empty plate. "I don't know. I guess I was afraid of you, Adam. As much as I wanted answers, I was still fearful to find out what role you may have played, if any, in Chelsea's disappearance."

Adam reached over and touched my hand. "I'm sorry if I frightened you that day...or any time after that, really. Scaring you has never been my intention."

I glanced up at him through my lashes. "I know that now." I sighed. "Although I have to admit it was all kind of exciting, too. Thinking you could be dangerous like that."

Adam shook his head. "Only you, Maddy... Only you would thrive on the possibility of that kind of danger."

Perhaps he was right. Oh hell, Adam was definitely right. My fear of him in those early days stoked my attraction to him.

Thinking of the first time Adam's lips touched mine, all those months ago, I quietly murmured, "Remember when you took me up to the lantern room?" I gestured to the iron staircase that spiraled up the inside of the lighthouse.

"Of course I remember," Adam replied. "That's where I first kissed you."

"Well, kind of," I corrected.

Adam raised an eyebrow. "Kind of, Maddy?"

"Yeah, your lips touched mine, true. But then stupid Nate called and interrupted everything."

"Ah, that's right." Adam's eyes met mine meaningfully. "Do you want to go up there now and I'll kiss you properly?"

I sure do! I cleared my throat and nodded demurely.

Five minutes later, Adam and I were up in the lantern room. Adam turned off the beacon so we'd not be blinded by the bright light. And wasting no time, he backed me up until I was pressed up against the storm panes.

The view to the outside was obscured by fog, just as it had been our first night up in the lantern room. Adam's lips brushed over mine, in the same soft way I remembered from that fall evening.

"Did it feel like this that first night?" Adam asked against my mouth.

I shook my head, my lips brushing his. "No," I breathily answered. "This is better."

And what was better improved further still. This night, unlike that first night, there were no interruptions from Nate. And light kisses soon turned into much, much more.

I was glad the fog obscured any potential view from the outside when my dress ended up a puddle of fabric on the floor. And I was even more thankful the storm panes were made of apparently very heavy glass. Because Adam Ward had no qualms about taking me right there at the top of the lighthouse, with my bare body pressed up to the glass.

What had started so many months ago had finally come full circle.

Chapter Twenty-One

May arrived, and Adam and I found ourselves heading down to Boston. The time for Trina and Walker's wedding had finally arrived.

With Helena and Nate accompanying us, we made the trip in Adam's private jet. Adam was the pilot, of course, and like our New Year's trip to Boston four months earlier, Nate chose to sit up in the cockpit with Adam, leaving Helena and I to make our own fun in the passenger area.

Helena's pregnancy precluded her from imbibing on alcoholic beverages, so she opted for sparkling apple cider when I broke out the wine glasses. Since I didn't really care to be the only person drinking on the flight, I also chose the cider.

Now, one might think the lack of alcohol might make for a boring flight...but no. Hell no, in fact. The nonalcoholic cider sent Helena and me into fits of giggles, same as if we'd been drinking alcohol.

"See, we don't need liquor to make us silly," I proclaimed, raising my almost-empty glass and swirling around what was left of the golden-toned liquid.

"It's all the damn sugar," Helena said, hiccupping.

"Give me that damn bottle." I reached for the empty cider bottle. "I want to see what's in this crap."

Helena handed me the bottle, and as I perused the label, I murmured, "Oh, jeez, it *is* loaded with sugar."

"Told you," Helena stated smugly.

And then I read off the nutritional info, or lack thereof. When I announced the amount of calories per glass, Helena moaned, "Oh great, just what I need, more calories. I already look like I'm six months pregnant. No one believes I'm only four months along."

Helena was showing—that was true—but she certainly did not appear to be six months pregnant. And nobody, to my knowledge, had thought her any further along than what she actually was.

"Oh, you're delusional," I said, rolling my eyes. "You look awesome, Helena. And you know it."

"I don't know about that, but thank you for saying so, Maddy." Helena suppressed a yawn as she finished speaking.

So much for the sugar high. Now my pregnant friend was just flat-out tired. I was a tad weary myself from all the laughing. Or maybe it was a post-sugar crash. In any case, Helena and I grew quiet and nodded off for the remainder of the flight.

Adam woke me up a short while later. "We've landed, Maddy," he said when I opened my eyes and stared at him, perplexed, as he knelt by my seat. "We're in Boston, babe."

"Oh, that's right," I said, yawning and stretching, "the wedding." I glanced around. "Where are Helena and Nate?"

"They're on their way to the hangar."

I patted the seat next to me where Helena had been sitting. "Sit with me for a minute, Adam. We may not get any time alone the rest of this weekend."

He sighed. "That's probably true."

Adam slipped into the seat next to me and leaned his head back against the headrest. I maneuvered in my seat until I was sideways, facing Adam with my legs tucked up under me. "The flight felt smooth," I said as I gestured to the cockpit. "Was everything okay up there?"

Adam turned his head, and our eyes met. "Yeah, it was pretty uneventful."

"So, are you excited for your sister's wedding?" I asked.

He rolled his eyes. "I'm happy for Trina and Walker, but big weddings aren't really my style."

Trina and Walker were having a huge wedding, like to the point that it was becoming the talk of the town. Impressive, since Boston was no small town. But Adam's sister and her husband-to-be were already society-page staples. We'd discovered that fact on New Year's Eve.

"I'm not really into the whole massive wedding thing, either," I admitted.

Adam cocked his head, his gaze watchful. "Do you want a small wedding then?"

I placed my hand on his and smiled. "Yeah, I do. I think I'd like that better than an extravagant wedding."

Adam agreed, and we spoke awhile longer about what each of us wanted from our impending nuptials. We were on the same page on almost everything. We even chose a date. The only thing we held differing opinions on was when to let everyone know what we'd decided.

"I think we should tell them tomorrow," I said, "so they can mark their calendars."

"You don't think it's too soon?" Adam asked, referring to the date we'd picked.

It seemed Adam wanted to give me more time to think about it. Like I'd ever decide I didn't want to marry him. *Silly man.*

I leaned across the seat and kissed him. "I love you, Adam. And I say the sooner I become Mrs. Adam Ward, the better."

Adam smiled. "Then it's decided."

And it was, so we sealed our decision with a kiss.

*

Trina and Walker were married in a huge, ornate cathedral, with nearly one thousand people in attendance. The reception afterward was held at a huge manor outside of Boston. The estate was packed, but Helena, Nate, Adam, and I sat together at an intimate corner table, along with Adam's parents.

Dr. and Mrs. Ward were beaming the entire day. Not only had their only daughter married the love of her life, but their only son had finally found happiness as well.

Adam's parents had been made aware of our engagement the day after it was official. And they'd been elated ever since.

"To Maddy and Adam," Dr. Ward stated as he raised his champagne glass. "I propose a toast... May the happiness in your soon-to-be entwined lives outweigh any strife in the days ahead, and may the love you so fortuitously found continue to grow stronger as the years pass."

There was a round of "hear, hears" and the clinking of glasses.

"So, have you thought about what time of the year you'd like to have this wedding, dear?" Adam's mom asked as she gently set her glass back down on the table.

Adam glanced my way and smiled. "I told you so," he mouthed, a reference to his prediction we'd face these kinds of questions today, particularly from his mother.

"Um..." I looked to Adam again for confirmation to share what we'd decided the day before in the plane.

When he nodded that I should continue, I told his mom we were thinking of an autumn wedding.

"Oh, how lovely," she said. "That's a fine time for a wedding. So, fall of next year, yes?"

"Uh, actually..."

Everyone at the table had apparently been listening in, for all eyes turned to me. I glanced to Adam once more, and he (thankfully) took over.

"Maddy and I are thinking of getting married *this* fall."

"Not next year?" Mrs. Ward asked her son, sounding somewhat bewildered.

Adam shook his head.

Helena, meanwhile, was smacking me in the arm. "Hey, you didn't say anything about getting married so soon. Not that I don't think it's a great idea."

"I think it's a great idea as well," Mrs. Ward suddenly piped in. Her expression had morphed from bewildered to very pleased.

"As do I," Dr. Ward added, smiling at his wife.

Clearly, both of Adam's parents were ready for Adam to get started on this new chapter of his life, a chapter that included me...and possibly grandchildren for them.

"Yeah, why wait?" Nate, who'd been quiet up until this point, chimed in.

"When it's right, it's right," Dr. Ward said.

While everyone around us clamored on and on about how wonderful it was there'd soon be another wedding to attend, Adam reached for my hand. "Do you want to dance, Madeleine?" he asked.

The music had been playing for a while, yet only a few people were on the dance floor.

"I'd like nothing more."

And even though there were hundreds of people in the huge ballroom, as Adam and I danced, bodies held close as a slow song played, it felt like the man I was going to marry and I were the only two people in the whole world.

Epilogue

Autumn arrived, splashing Maine in splendid colors. Fade Island was awash in shades of red, plum, and gold. I found the isle more beautiful than the year before, when I'd first arrived with the intention of solving a mystery. When I thought about it now, I couldn't believe how much had happened in one year's time.

Not one, but *two* mysteries had been solved, Adam was targeted for assassination, and I'd been run down by a crazed psychopath.

And those were just a few of the mystery-related things.

My personal life had changed in many ways as well. I'd renewed family ties, rediscovered old friendships, and made new friends. But most importantly, I found love... with Adam Ward.

From the moment we first saw one another again, in Adam's living room after I'd trespassed on his property, Adam and I were on a trajectory to this day—our wedding day.

And here it was...

As I held onto my father's arm, I took in the touching scene before me.

High above a raging sea, on a large, flat stretch of grassy land, Adam stood waiting for me at an altar that had been erected near the edge of a cliff on his estate property.

The man I was about to marry looked insanely handsome, as always. It was no surprise then when my breath caught in my throat as Adam smiled at me.

I faltered a little. But my father, at my side, kept me right.

"Are you okay, sweetheart?" Dad whispered as we walked along a snow-white runner that was dappled in autumn-toned rose petals. The thrum of "The Wedding March" played softly in the background.

"I'm fine, Dad," I whispered back.

And I was fine, better than fine. I just couldn't believe my dream was coming true. I was about to become Adam Ward's wife.

All of our friends and families were in attendance to witness the happy event, seated in rows of ivory-colored chairs. They smiled encouragingly as I made my way down the aisle, the long train of my silk wedding gown rustling through the strewn petals.

I'd never felt so happy and loved. Not just by Adam, but by my father at my side, as well as the people in the seats.

As I made my way to Adam, I smiled as I walked by his parents, as well as his sister, Trina, and her new husband, Walker. Erin and Stowe, who'd flown up from Boston, gave a little wave from the far end of the row. Max lifted his hand and gave me a thumbs-up. And my brother, Brent, on the opposite side of the aisle winked encouragingly as I passed. His wife sat next to him, and beyond her, Helena's mom.

Helena's mom's was cradling Helena and Nate's newborn baby boy, who was swaddled in a blanket of blue. Little Nathan had been born two weeks early, but he was healthy as could be. He let out a small cry, and Helena, my maid of honor, beamed proudly as her eyes moved to her baby. Nate, Adam's best man, looked pretty damn proud himself as he glanced over to where Helena's mom was rocking the baby in her arms, trying to quiet him.

When we reached the altar, my dad placed my hand in Adam's. "Be good to my daughter," he murmured.

Adam squeezed my hand gently, and said to my dad, "I will, Mayor Fitch, I promise. I plan to love and honor Maddy every day for the rest of our lives."

Adam's serene blue eyes then met mine. And before we even recited the vows we'd written for one another, I knew in my heart that Adam would do as he promised: he'd be good to me. Of course, I planned to be very good to him as well.

While the reverend officiating welcomed everyone to our wedding, Adam held my gaze. "Forever," he murmured quietly.

I whispered back, "Forever, Adam. Forever."

The End

Acknowledgments

Thank you to my family and friends, for all the love and support from the very beginning of this journey. Thank you to all the bloggers who read and review my novels and do such a phenomenal job of getting the word out. Thank you to Damon for creating great covers and Benjamin for superb print and e-book layouts. And thank you, readers, for making all the work that goes into a novel worthwhile.

Feel free to contact me. I love hearing from readers.

Goodreads Author Page:
http://www.goodreads.com/author/
show/6433082.S_R_Grey

Facebook:
https://www.facebook.com/pages/
SR-Grey/361159217278943

Twitter:
https://twitter.com/AuthorSRGrey

Pinterest:
http://www.pinterest.com/srgrey/

Author Bio

S.R. Grey is the author of the bestselling novel Harbour Falls, as well as Willow Point and Wickingham Way, all novels in A Harbour Falls Mystery series. She is also the author of I Stand Before You, the first novel in the Judge Me Not series.

Ms. Grey resides in western Pennsylvania. She has a Bachelor of Science in Business Administration degree, as well as an MBA. Her background is in business, but her passion lies in writing.

She is currently working on Never Doubt Me, the second novel of the Judge Me Not series. Expected publication: Spring 2014.

I Stand Before You *is the first novel of*
S.R. Grey's newest series, Never Doubt Me.

Read the first chapter here…

Prologue

Chase

I lean my head back against the headrest, crank the passenger window down the rest of the way. The June night air rustles through my hair, reminding me I desperately need a trim. I run my fingers through the strands, chasing the path of the breeze.

My grandmother likes to lecture that I shouldn't have hair sticking out at odd angles, strands curling at the nape of my neck.

"You're such a handsome young man, Chase," Grandma Gartner said just this morning, *tsk*ing when I sat down for breakfast. "You look so much like your father did when he was your age. But, you know, *he* always kept *his* hair short and tidy." And then there was a pause, a long, dramatic sigh. She set down a plate of eggs—over easy—in front of me. "My poor Jack. God rest his soul." My grandmother crossed herself.

Her poor Jack, my father with the short and tidy hair—dead and gone.

I thought: *I am not my dad, Gram. He failed us, he gave up on us.* But the words never passed my lips. And they never will. Hearing them would only hurt my grandmother's feelings and she's too good to hear the angry thoughts poisoning my polluted mind. So I keep all that shit locked deep inside.

This morning was no different. I kept things light, said something like, "The girls like my hair like this, Gram. Got to keep the ladies happy, ya know."

Then I ducked and waited for the inevitable swat with the dish towel. But it never came. Instead, the lines in my grandmother's face deepened.

"You don't need to be concerning yourself with keeping ladies happy, young man. You're only twenty. Messing with women at your age will only lead to trouble."

I knew what she meant this morning, and I know it now too. She's worried I'll end up getting some girl pregnant. Then I'll be fucked, well and good. But I'm always careful, take the necessary precautions. Besides, it isn't my womanizing ways that's becoming a problem. If only. No, unfortunately, it's my ever-growing dependency on drugs—something my grandmother would never suspect—that has me worried these days.

These days… Yeah, right. More like these blurry, fucked-up segments of time.

Sighing, I roll the window up just enough to lean my head against the cool glass. *What am I going to do?* I silently ask myself.

What I really need to do is get the hell out of this tiny Ohio farm town I landed back in two years ago. I'm spinning my wheels here in Harmony Creek, hanging with a bad crowd. Problem is I have no plan, no money either. Drugs are my escape and have been for quite a while. My priorities are all fucked up. My life, it's upside down. Every day it seems like getting high—and staying that way—is my only goal. I want to stop—believe me I do—but I don't think I know how to anymore.

A lump forms in my throat at this thought, but I swallow it down. "Hey," I say to Tate, who is driving. "Let's get out of this town."

Tate Cody, my friend…and my partner in crime in everything wild and crazy these days—women, drugs, drinking, fighting—you name it, we do it. And if we're not doing it nowadays, chances are we've done it at least once over the past couple of years. We've yet to slow down; we live on the edge.

I sometimes wonder when we'll fall.

"What do you think we're doing, Chase, my man?"

I take in and process Tate's reply, while he lifts a bottle of cheap gin to his lips and hits the gas. And for this one long, tortuous drawn-out second, I can't make a distinction between what I asked Tate and what I was only thinking. I panic, assuming my partner in crime's response is to let me know it's finally happening, we're really falling.

But then Tate adds, "I'm getting us out of here as fast as I can," and I breathe a little easier. He just means we're leaving Harmony Creek. Not falling, after all. *Shit, I need to ease up on the drugs.*

I glance out the window, and though it's dark I can see we're heading east, nearing the state line. Soon we'll be out of Ohio completely, and in the neighboring state of Pennsylvania. That's where we're supposed to hook up with two girls tonight. They're from New Castle, and we're meeting at a lake across the state line.

I don't really care about all that, though. What I'd really rather do is keep on going. Hop on Interstate 80 and clock the miles to Jersey. Better yet, Tate and I could go farther. We could drive our asses straight into New York-fucking-City. Now that would be sweet.

So while Tate barrels down a back road the police rarely patrol—until you get into Pennsylvania, that is—I pretend we're leaving Harmony Creek for good. No looking back, no regrets, just flying the fuck out of this lame-ass small town.

And speaking of flying, I'm flying a bit now too, feeling fine, baby, fine. I close my eyes so I can savor the s-l-o-w creep of numbness that cocoons me like a warm and fuzzy blanket.

I feel nothing, yet I feel everything.

My skin tingles a little, but when I touch my hand to my face it feels detached, like these parts of my body belong to two different people, neither of them me. That thought makes me happy, escape is exactly what I crave.

Needless to say, I've smoked—a lot—and not just weed. But it's the pills I swallowed a while ago that are starting to wrap me up and spin me the fuck out.

A bottle hits the back of my hand and my eyes fly open. Shit, I forgot I am not alone in this car.

"Drink, fucker," Tate urges.

I take the gin, despite the fact I can barely see straight. *No* isn't part of my vocabulary when I'm like this. And, sadly, more often than not, this is exactly how I am. This is who I am becoming: Chase Gartner, burgeoning drug addict.

As per most nights, Tate and I stopped at Kyle's before embarking on *this* night's little adventure. Kyle Tanner supplies us with more drugs than we could ever hope for. And the quality is always top notch. Kyle takes a certain kind of pride in dealing only primo product. But you'd never guess such a thing if you saw the rundown shithole he lives in.

Our dealer resides on the *other* side of town, over by the closed-down glass factory, in a clapboard house he shares with his meth-addicted dad. Lately, going there has been a contradiction of emotions for me. I love and hate concurrently when Tate and I cross over the railroad tracks that mark the end of the safe neighborhoods of Harmony Creek. Then, I vacillate between love and hate as I watch the Sparkle Mart grocery store appear...then disappear. I lean a little more towards hate when we reach the run-down apartment building where the junkies hang out, where their emaciated bodies lean lazily against the dirty brick exterior.

I sure as fuck don't want to end up there, God, no. But maybe I'm powerless to stop my downward spiral. Lord knows, by the time we start down the long dirt road that leads to Kyle's place, I crave and I want. And love trumps hate by that point. Even the junkies seem less scary. So we go...and we go...and we keep going back.

Tate tells me the road to Kyle's house is the road to salvation. *Salvation, my ass.* I'd be more inclined to say Tate and I are traveling a path to hell. We're in the express lane to damnation, and one step closer to burning every time we travel down that fucking dirt road. I know it, he knows it, but do we ever do anything to stop? Do we try to crawl out of the hole we're wallowing in? No, never.

In fact, Tate wants us to delve in deeper—start selling. He says we'll make, at the minimum, enough money to help pay for the copious amounts of shit we ingest... snort...smoke. Yeah, we do it all, everything short of needles. I somehow know if I ever cross *that* line, there will be no going back.

But I'm considering the selling thing, albeit for a different reason than my friend. Tate hopes to eventually make enough cash to buy his own wheels. He hates borrowing the piece of shit we're currently in—his mom's old, rusted Ford Focus. I just want to make enough money to buy a ticket out of this place. The little bit I earn painting people's houses, picking up construction work here and there—it's not adding up fast enough for my liking.

Hell, I still live at my grandmother's farmhouse out on Cold Springs Lane. Granted, I recently fixed up the little apartment above the detached garage, moved from a bedroom in the main house to an area not too much larger. But that little apartment provides privacy, and that's what I need. I am no longer a teenager, like when I first moved back two years ago. That's why I want, more than anything, to just get the fuck out of here. I'm thinking the money I make selling will make escape a reality, not just some pipe dream. No pun intended.

I raise the bottle of gin to my lips and tip it back. Alcohol heats my throat. "I think I'm going to take Kyle up on his offer," I say after I swallow the burn, the resulting grimace distorting my voice. "I need the money and it's going to take forever to earn it legit."

"You're making the right decision, my friend," Tate replies as he reaches over to take back the bottle.

Whoa... My vision turns wonky. There are three overlapping filmy images of my friend, and then just two.

"It's all about the numbers, man," two filmy Tates tell me.

I tell myself I need to slow down, and then I say to Tate, "That it is." I squeeze my eyes shut to keep from swaying in my seat. "That it is," I repeat.

The irony is that I once had money. Well, my family did, enough that my parents had a trust fund set up for me. Not a big one, mind you, but enough that it would've allowed for me to go to a decent college, get set up in a new city, shit like that.

I have no idea what my future holds nowadays, but I know it's been tainted by my past.

Back when I was around eight my parents moved from this town out to Las Vegas. My dad, who'd been successfully building houses here for a while, started a similar construction business out in Nevada. The timing was right, the stars aligned. We caught magic in the early days of the housing boom. Everything was golden and money poured in. It was happy times. For a while.

During those good times, Mom got pregnant. She gave me a little brother named Will that I still love like crazy and miss every fucking day. We used to talk on the phone all the time, but now I'm lucky if I get a two-word text from my little bro. I suppose when you're eleven years old—and haven't seen your big brother in two years—memories become a little hazy.

That's another thing the extra money from selling drugs will help with: I'll have enough funds to fly out to Vegas to see Will. Or I can just buy him a ticket to come here. As it is my mom, Abby, barely makes enough to get by out there.

But, like I said before, it wasn't always that way. In the early years, my father's construction company grew and thrived, so much so that I once entertained dreams of taking over the business. I used to imagine following in my father's footsteps, as sons are apt to do.

One afternoon, when I was about thirteen, I told my dad I wanted to build homes, same as he did. I showed him some sketches, just some basic designs and floor plans I'd thrown together. My dad was impressed. And not the false kind of fawning parents often try to sell to their kids. No, my drawings truly floored Jack Gartner. I could tell he couldn't believe his eldest son possessed that kind of crazy talent. He told me I should aim high, the sky was the limit. My sketches were incredible, he said, especially for my age. I could be an architect if I wanted, design skyscrapers even.

I had no reason not to believe him.

When you're thirteen you think you can have it all. Life hasn't roughed you up so very much...yet. At least it hadn't for me. So I told my father I'd do both—I would design the skyscrapers, and then I'd build them. My buildings would sell like hotcakes, and I'd be as rich as Donald Trump. No, richer even.

"The sky's the limit," I said, echoing my father's words back to him.

Dad smiled and patted me on the back.

Jack Gartner wasn't patronizing me, he truly believed in my possibility. "You have talent, Chase," he said. "Just don't ever lose yourself. If you can stay true to your dream...to who you are...then you'll do more than fly. Someday you'll soar."

Yeah, right. I sure am soaring at the moment, but I have a feeling this isn't what Dad had in mind.

Tate tries to pass the bottle back to me, but my mood has dampened. The pills, along with the memories, are doing a fucking number on my emotions. I'm sad one minute, reflective the next, mad at everything, contemplative over nothing. I guess I am officially fucked up.

I push the bottle away, harder than necessary, and clear liquid sloshes over the side. "Asshole," Tate mutters.

"Sorry," I say.

Do I really mean it? No, it's just a word, an empty string of letters. Empty, like me.

I tune Tate out. I am high as fuck and lost in my mind. We idle at a swinging red light hanging over an empty, dark stretch of road, and I sit waiting on an imaginary red light in my head, one on memory-fucking-lane.

When I blink, both lights turn green...

My dad started taking me to work the summer I showed him the drawings. I learned how to wire a home, how to put in plumbing, how to lay insulation. And that was just the beginning. I used to watch how my dad talked to the guys. He treated them with respect, and in turn they went the extra mile for him. It was all "Yes sir, Mr. Gartner," "Consider it done, Jack."

When I turned fourteen, my dad bought me a drafting table, a bunch of fancy software too. The kind real architects use, or so he said. I practiced all the time, got pretty damn good. I was building my wings, you see, preparing to fly.

Will was only five, but damn if that kid didn't love to sit around and watch me sketch. For him, I'd draw all kinds of ridiculous structures.

"Dwaw me a house, Chasey," he asked this one day.

I laughed while I tousled his blond hair. I remember the fine strands looked so light in the sunlit room. Hell, they were almost white. "All right, buddy, what kind do you want?"

"A house like a tweeeee," Will sing-song replied, green eyes innocent and wide as he focused on the sketch pad I'd picked up from my desk.

I readied a colored pencil and asked for clarification, "Okay, a tree house, right?"

"No-o-o." Will shook his little head vociferously. "A house that *is* a twee, Chasey."

"Aha, got it," I said.

And I did. I drew Will a tree house shaped exactly like a tree, big, sturdy, loaded down with bushy branches. The leaves I shaded in the color of my brother's eyes. I sketched a door at the base of the trunk, then drew a Will-sized truck and parked it under a low-lying branch. After I finished with some final shading, I held the drawing up for my brother to see.

Will's house looked like one of those tree houses in the commercials with the elves and the cookies, only this one I'd drawn was far better. There was a lot more detail, and I'd drawn the tree in 2-D. In among the branches and the leaves all the rooms were in cross-section, done up in varying shades of blue, Will's favorite color. I also made certain every last blue-shaded 2D-room overflowed with toys.

Will threw his arms around my neck and told me he loved his *twee house*. Then, he leaned back and told me he loved *me* even more.

He gave me a kiss on my cheek. That shit always touched my heart, choked me up a little. "I love you too, buddy," was about all I could say as I held on to a little boy who meant the world to me.

Things are never bad when love is abundant. I thought it would stay that way forever, I did. A home filled with love, a happy family, just a good and easy life.

Man, was I ever wrong.

Shortly after I turned seventeen my world began to crumble. The bottom fell out of the housing market. The wave everyone was riding touched the surf and crashed. My dad's business was one of the first to fail. He had over-extended himself; all our assets were mortgaged. He made ridiculous deals, attempting to keep us afloat, but his efforts proved futile. We sunk faster than a stone.

I sold the fancy architect software on eBay, the drafting table too. I gave the money to my parents, but it was merely a drop in the bucket compared to what we owed. I watched my once-vibrant dad turn into a shadow of the man he once was. My mom, always so young-looking and pretty, developed dark circles under her eyes—from crying, worrying, not being able to sleep. She even tried her hand at the casinos, we were that fucking desperate. But everyone knows gambling is a loser's game. The house always wins in the end.

One night, my mom was at one of those casinos. It wasn't the first time she'd spent hours and hours away, trying to win back what we'd lost. She came out ahead a little here and there, but it was never enough, never enough.

Will had fallen asleep early that night, so my dad and I were more or less alone. He asked me if I was hungry. When I nodded slowly, reluctant to reveal just how ravenous I really was and cause my father any additional undue guilt, he sighed, picked up the phone, and ordered a bunch of Chinese take-out.

I swear I smelled that food before the delivery man even pulled up to the house. Beef Chow Mein, General Tso's chicken, Hot and Sour soup, and eggrolls, the first real meal I'd eaten in weeks. And even though my dad and I had to sit on the floor—our furniture had been repossessed days earlier—I savored every fucking bite.

Afterward, my dad said he had somewhere to go. There was something he had to do. Would I keep an eye on Will?

"Sure," I told him while shoving white take-out cartons with little metal handles— leftovers I'd saved for Will and Mom—into the fridge.

With my father gone, I had nothing to do. Our TVs were gone, the stereos too. Video games? Forget it. Those were among the first things to go. So, I wandered around the house barefoot, padding around on neglected hardwood floors. I trudged from one empty room to the next.

Then I took a minute to look in on Will.

My little brother slept on an air mattress in the middle of his now-barren room. The *twee house* sketch, the only thing left on his four stark walls, had fallen. It lay abandoned on the floor, close to Will's hand, close to where his little arm was dangling off the side of the mattress. To me, it looked as if my brother was subconsciously reaching for the drawing. Three years had passed since I'd drawn Will's tree house— and I'd sketched hundreds of other things for him since that sunny day—but that particular piece of made-with-love art was still my brother's favorite. I think to him it symbolized something more. He'd once said my sketch gave him hope. I guess it reminded him of when things were good.

I stepped into his dark room and picked up Will's hope. I kissed the top of his head and gently placed his *twee house* next to his sleeping form. I made my way back down to the living room, feeling solemn and too fucking worn for seventeen. Tears welled in my eyes, but I refused to let them fall. *Hell with that shit.* The paper bag that had held the Chinese food was still on the floor. Frustrated, I kicked it out of my way. A fortune cookie shot out and landed at my feet. I picked the projectile up, ripped the plastic covering off, and slid a tiny piece of paper from the confines of the cookie.

The fortune stayed in my hand, the cookie ended up in my mouth.

Truthfully, I was still hungry. Crunching away and savoring sugary goodness, I read the words on the little slip of paper I held between my fingers.

As I stand before you, judge me not.

It sounded a little hokey and I almost threw the fortune away. But there was something about those words that made me hesitate, something almost prescient. I ended up folding the little piece of paper in half and tucking it in to my pocket. Maybe I needed some symbol of hope just like my brother. I knew the things happening in my life would eventually define my future, and I guess I hoped no matter what occurred those things wouldn't ultimately define me.

My mom came back later that night, but my dad never did.

Jack Gartner had gotten on route 160, heading west to California. But he never made it out of Nevada. His car was found at the bottom of a ravine, below what the officers who came to our door to break the news termed *a treacherous curve*.

Killed on impact, we were told.

Did he lose control, or drive off the road on purpose? Maybe his plan all along had been to leave us and start a new life in California. That's what my mom believed at the time. Still does, in fact.

I, however, am not so sure. My father didn't pack a thing. Sixty dollars and a cancelled credit card, that's all he had on him. I think my dad just gave up. He quit on us, and that was the way he chose to end it. My mom can delude herself all she wants, but I know in my heart that I'm the one who's got it right.

Anyway, the bank took the house soon after my father's death. My mom sold off what little was left. For awhile, we became nomads in the desert. We lived in the only big-ticket item that hadn't been repossessed, a white minivan. The Honda Odyssey was home…until Mom won enough money gambling to move us into a cheap apartment. Our new residence was a dump, but at least it had running water. And it was furnished. Kind of.

When we first stepped across the threshold and Mom caught me scowling at the rusty fixtures, the water-stained ceiling, the musty olive-green carpeting, she tried hard to convince me our new place had its good points.

"Like what?" I asked.

"It's close to The Strip. That'll be convenient."

"Convenient for who?" I sniped. "You?"

"Chase," she said pointedly, "it's better than living in a minivan."

She had a point there, so we moved in the next day. Will's first reaction was to run straight to one of the two back bedrooms and hang up his tattered *twee house* sketch. I followed him and watched as he stood on a soiled mattress on the floor—in a shoebox of a room we were going to have to share—and pinned hope on a wall.

After we were settled, time, as it does, marched on. Will and I attended school, while my mom—still fevered and sick with the gambling virus—spent her days in the casinos.

I turned eighteen that April. But no one really noticed. Well, Will did. Not much got by that kid.

He stuck a candle he found in the back of a drawer in the kitchen on a stale snack cake. He made me sit on the only kitchen chair that didn't rock when you shifted, and then he placed the snack cake on a card table we used as a kitchen table.

Will sang me the most beautiful off-key and from-the-heart rendition of "Happy Birthday" that I have ever heard, before or since. When he was done, I leaned forward to blow out the candle. Will stopped me and told me to make a wish first, so I did. And then I blew out the candle. Will clapped and cheered. He asked me what I wished for and I told him it was a secret. I didn't want to tell him I wished for him to be given a better life than what we were, at the time, living. My brother and I split the snack cake in two, dinner for the night, and ate in contemplative silence.

Summer arrived that year and I somehow managed to graduate. But—with my trust fund long gone—college was no longer on the table. With no real guidance, and a lot of pent-up frustration, my downward slide took hold. I was angry all the time, and ended up getting into too many fights to count. The places in Vegas where I'd started hanging were tough. Early on, I got my ass kicked...often.

But then something happened.

I learned how to use my strength, my quickness, *and* my anger. I started to win. I had a real knack for fighting and rapidly turned into a badass nobody messed with. I earned street cred. All that really meant was guys started showing me respect and girls suddenly wanted to have sex with me. I happily obliged more than a few of the latter.

But all that shit meant nothing, I was empty inside. I had no one to talk to about the mixed-up emotions I didn't know how to deal with. Like, why was I so angry all the time? Why did I like to fight so much? Why did it feel so good to make someone else hurt?

But mostly I wondered why I missed my dad so much.

I missed talking to my father, seeing his face everyday. I had relied on him, I still needed him. But he was gone. He took his own life. Why couldn't I just accept what had happened and forget him?

But I couldn't, and, worse yet, I longed for answers.

Every day, for a while, in my quest for enlightenment, I'd grab the bus outside our apartment and visit my father. Well, I'd visit his grave. At the head of where my father rested eternally, I'd sit under a big stone angel kneeling by his grave—thankful for the little bit of shade she offered under the hot, beating sun of the desert.

Sweaty and lost, I'd ask her if she could tell me why my dad wasn't still alive. Why had God allowed Dad to take himself away? Why did my father choose to leave me? Why would he leave Mom and Will too? Was our love not enough for him? Did he regret his decision when he realized there was no going back?

Of course, the stone angel had no answers, and one day I just quit going. No more sitting in the shadow of the angel, no more hot and beating sun. No more asking questions that could never be answered.

My trips to the cemetery were over, but that didn't mean I wanted to forget that *someone*—even though he'd left— had once believed in me. Despite everything, I still loved my father and part of me yearned to be just like him.

So, July of that year, I had his angel's likeness—the stone one at his grave—inked in profile on the middle of my upper back, between my shoulder blades.

I shift in the passenger seat now.

I can almost feel her back there, watching over me, like my dad's angel watches over him. And like his angel, mine is kneeling. The edges of her heavy robe lie in a puddle of fabric around her. Her wings are folded against her back. Her hair is long, obscuring the side of her face. And her head is bowed. In supplication or in shame, I haven't decided which. But if she's been watching the shit I've been doing these past two years, it's probably in shame.

After the angel tat healed, Mom hit for more money. I successfully talked her into paying for another tattoo, guilted her into it really. In any case, I ended up with big, intricately detailed wings inked up and over my shoulder blades. The top feathers curve onto my shoulders, while the wings dip down the sides of my back, effectively framing the angel.

But the angel and the wings weren't enough. I wanted something more to remember my father, something to remind me always of that final night, when it was just him and me, eating Chinese food on the floor of an empty home, a last supper shared.

I kept coming back to the cookie, the fortune inside, the hope it symbolized.

As I stand before you, judge me not.

Words printed on a piece of paper, but really they were so much more. So I had those words inked—in concise and script letters—around my left bicep.

My tats were but temporal attempts to heal my soul, as my heart remained an open wound. There was no solace to be had at home. In fact, things were getting worse. I started to drink and do drugs to ease the pain and fill the void. I hated what had happened to our family. Seeing Will transformed from an energetic little boy to a sullen nine-year-old left me sad and frustrated. And watching my mother try to heal her fractured heart with gambling—and eventually men—just pissed me the fuck off.

But at least Mom wasn't indulging in one-night stands like I'd been doing. Nope, Abby actually went out on dates. Still, her attempt at dating led to a revolving door of boyfriends. Some lasted a week or two, some a little longer, but the one common denominator they all shared was that not a single one liked me.

Mom told me to try harder, give these guys a chance for her sake. I laughed and told Abby her men could blow me. "Chase, don't be crude," was her response.

By the end of the summer Mom hooked up with what turned out to be steady boyfriend number three. I was no fool; I immediately sensed my days were numbered. I would've had to have been blind not to see the writing on the wall, a wall I didn't realize I was hurtling toward. But it wasn't just Abby's lame new boyfriend disliking me that was a problem. There was something else, something she'd never admit to. There was no escaping it though, not really.

I saw Abby's problem every day when I looked in the mirror.

Standing in a cramped and steam-filled bathroom, hot water running, can of shave cream poised in hand, I couldn't deny the truth in front of me. I'd swipe at the misted mirror with my free hand, leaving it streaky, but mostly clear. And it wasn't me I saw in the reflection, it was my father. That's how much I looked like Jack Gartner, even at eighteen. And *that* was my mother's real problem.

Shit. Even thinking about it now—two years later— fucks with my head.

I glance over at Tate. He's quiet, taking long pulls from the bottle. I shift in my seat and wind up the window the rest of the way. Time to assess my bleary reflection, time to compare it to what it was, time to compare it to the man who made me...I sometimes do this just to fuck with myself.

When I take in my reflection, I laugh. Hell, the resemblance is still uncanny. And just like when I used to stare at the steamed-up mirror in the bathroom, it's my dad's eyes staring back at me now. But these pale blues are all mine. Yeah, *his* whites were never shot with red like mine.

Still, even with the bloodshot eyes, similarities far outweigh differences. Though it's not *short and tidy*—like Grandma Gartner would like it to be—my hair is the exact same shade as her son's once was, light brown. Jack also blessed me with his straight nose, his square jaw, and his defined cheekbones. Everyone used to say my dad was good-looking, I guess I am too. Girls seem to think so, that's for sure. And my mother sure was smitten with my dad.

Abby used to lean across the front seat of the sporty car my dad bought for himself during the good times. Will and

I would be in the back, rolling our eyes at each other. My mom would kiss my dad, making him swerve a little as he drove. She'd tell him he was gorgeous, and that she loved him. Dad would laugh and tell Abby he loved her even more. He'd say his love for her burned hotter than the Vegas sun above us. My mom loved that shit. Will and I, however, would groan in disgust and make gagging noises.

Shit, I feel like gagging now. Not because of the memory, but at how closely I still resemble my dead father. I turn away from my reflection. I can't bear to endure this self-inflicted torture any longer. No wonder I was fucking sent away. Too bad I couldn't disappear completely just as easily right now. Guess, in a way, that's why I live my life the way I do, filling it with drugs...sex...violence.

Back then my very presence in my mom's life must have been a constant reminder of all she had lost. When you're striving to move on, you don't need an anchor to the past. She could move forward with Will, he was just a kid. Besides, he looked like her, not like my father. But I was eighteen, an adult, and far too much my father's son for everyone's comfort. I guess it was just too difficult for Mom to look at me—see *him*—and be reminded of all she'd once had.

So the day steady boyfriend number three, a guy named Gary, told her she could move in with him, I kind of fucking knew the invitation wouldn't be extended to me.

Sure enough, on a blistering hot afternoon, my mom sent Will out to ride his bike and told me we had to talk. She sat me down on the ratty couch in our shitty apartment. I felt like a condemned man waiting to hear his fate, and all the while the noisy air conditioning unit in the window behind me kept blowing gusts of lukewarm air across the back of my neck.

Not that it mattered. I barely noticed. I was mostly numb. In preparation for this "talk," I'd done a couple of lines of coke in my room. Of course, I hadn't brought that shit out until after Will had left. One thing I stuck to was that I never let my little brother see me taking part in any of my newfound vices.

Anyway, that day in the living room, I couldn't sit still. Fidgeting, fidgeting, tapping my foot. Mom took no notice, she was almost as bad. Pacing back and forth in front of me, smoking a cigarette, a new habit she'd just acquired. Gary smoked, so she'd picked up the habit too. *Pathetic*, I remember thinking.

My mother appeared so edgy and wired I almost asked her if she was dabbling in drugs, like me, or if what she had to say was really just that fucking bad. She started speaking before I ever got the chance.

"You're not a kid anymore, Chase," she began, still pacing, ashes peppering the olive-green carpeting.

She took a drag, crinkled her brow, and leaned over to stub her cigarette out in a plastic ashtray on a low table.

"You have to get started on doing something, somewhere, kid," she said as she spun to face me.

She stood right in front of me, and though my head was down I watched her every move. She blew out a breath and I watched her dark blonde bangs lift up off her forehead. A few strands stuck to her skin. Mom was starting to sweat.

"So, Grandma Gartner called the other day," she continued, her words deliberate, pointed, like a knife. "She said she's got lots of room in that old farmhouse back in Ohio. And she sure could use some company."

I looked up at her in disbelief. This woman who'd given me life tried to smile, but she could not. She knew damn well she was spewing pure bullshit. She just wanted rid of me.

"Just spit it out," I ground through clenched teeth, my voice far from even.

"Okay, of course, honey." She looked everywhere but at me. "Uh, so, Gram thinks moving back to Harmony Creek might do you some good, get you out of Vegas, give you a chance to start over, and—"

"Mom, I'm only eighteen. Start over?" I blew out a quick breath. "I haven't even had a chance to get started *here*."

Her expression grew stern. "Chase, don't act like I don't know the things you do behind my back." I tried to protest, but she shushed me. "I know you use drugs. I know you bring girls back when Will's not around. That shit isn't going to fly once we move in with Gary. He won't stand for it, Chase. He has standards—"

I snorted, "The fuck he does—"

"I'm not going to argue with you about it," she said, her voice tired and cracking.

When she reached for her pack of cigarettes, I noticed her hands were shaking. "Honey, I just think Grandma Gartner's is the best place for you right now, okay?"

I picked at a hole in my jeans. "Do I have a choice?" I asked, defeated, and, truthfully, feeling like I'd just been set adrift.

She shook her head no.

I'd known it was coming, but her words still flayed me up the middle and pierced my already damaged heart. I was shocked that my heart could continue beating, since it felt all smashed to hell. But beat it did. In fact, my heart pumped faster and faster, like it was going to burst right out of my fucking chest. Whether my reaction was from cocaine...or despair...I couldn't quite figure.

With my heart pounding like a sped-up death knell, I tried to push some words out of my cotton-dry mouth. "Mom..." I croaked, my voice catching.

I just couldn't finish.

Verbal communication failed me, so I tried to meet her eyes, speak to her soul. Was this really what she wanted? Send her eldest son away? Give up on me? Just like Dad did with all of us.

I searched and searched, but my mother had no answers in her big green eyes, no more than the stone angel had at my father's grave.

Abby took in a stuttered breath and turned away. She swiped at a tear. "It's for the best, Chase," she mumbled.

And then she left me sitting there, all alone, warm air blowing across the back of my neck.

I went back to my room and cut up three more lines.

That was nearly two years ago and here I am. Mom is still in Las Vegas with Will, on steady boyfriend number six, last I heard. She's still chasing the elusive jackpot too, hoping to recapture the life she once knew.

Good luck with that, I think bitterly. *Jackpot, my ass*. If anyone needs to hit a fucking jackpot, it's me.

Suddenly, drug-induced visions of flashing pots of gold swim lazily into my head, along with some break-dancing leprechauns, and I can't help but chuckle.

Tate looks over. He must think my mood has improved, 'cause he starts talking all excitedly about how much money we're going to make from our new business venture with Kyle. I listen to his voice, not really hearing any words, but then the cell buzzes and I am alert, very alert.

Tate tosses it my way. "That there would be the ladies," he says—all smooth like—as I catch the cell with one hand. Even impaired, my coordination is impeccable.

"Ladies, my ass." I roll my eyes.

Tate laughs, knowing as well as I do that the two girls we're meeting up with tonight are no ladies. They're looking for the same thing we are, but therein lies the beauty.

"What's it say?" he asks, nodding to the cell.

The text is kind of blurry, but, then again, everything is. I blink a few times and my vision clears. When I read it out loud, I mimic a high-pitched girl's voice, just to be an ass. "Crystal and I are almost at the lake. Come prepared. Tammy. Laugh out loud, winking smiley face."

"Dude-e-e." Tate shoots me a knowing sidelong glance. "You know what *come prepared* means, right? You got that covered, yeah?"

As reckless as I am—and that's pretty fucking reckless—I always make sure I wrap my shit up. Better safe than sorry. But as I feel around in the pockets of my jeans I realize I've left the condoms at home. "Fuck," I mutter.

The blue *Welcome to Pennsylvania* sign looms ahead, our headlights flashing off the reflective letters.

Tate asks, "What?"

I rake my fingers through my hair. "I forgot the goddamn things at home."

"Not a problem. We'll just stop at the convenience store across the state line."

"Bad idea," I counter. "Cops are always hanging out in there. You think they won't notice how fucked up we are?"

"How fucked up *you* are," Tate corrects, laughing. "I didn't smoke nearly as much as you."

"You smoked plenty," I mumble under my breath.

But Tate is right, I smoked more. And Tate smoked only weed. Plus, my friend didn't see the pills Kyle slipped me before we left.

Still, I nod to the almost-empty bottle. "You pretty much drank that whole thing, dickhead. You'll never pass a field sobriety test."

"Yeah, but I don't plan on taking one, my friend. And, I hide it better than you." He shrugs. "Trust me, I got it covered. Just wait in the car. It'll only take a sec."

Tate's always confident like this. He can talk anyone into just about anything. I always tell him he's a natural-born salesman. Maybe if we ever get our shit together he can do something legit using his smooth ways. It's cool, it's Tate's thing, and it helps make him popular. He's an okay-looking guy—brown hair, brown eyes, kind of skinny—but it's his smooth talk that gets him in with the girls. They eat that shit up.

We cross the state line, turn into the convenience store. No cop cars. "See, we're good," Tate says, still as confident as ever.

I flip up my black hoodie hood and slouch down in my seat. "Just be quick," I mumble.

Tate hesitates, and I know something is up. "What the fuck are you waiting for?" I ask.

He begins his sentence with "Don't be pissed—" and I cut him off right away, hoping I won't have to kick my good friend's skinny ass. It would be a damn shame really, since Tate wouldn't stand a chance against the likes of me. I am way bigger and far stronger, and the rage within me has no match.

"What?" I spit out, clenching my jaw.

Tate ignores my attitude; he's used to it. "I kind of need you to hold on to something while I go in there. Just in case."

"Just in case of what?"

I am running out of patience. I scrub my hand down my face, wary to hear what Tate the salesman is up to now.

He smirks, and I tell him to knock that shit off, save it for the "ladies."

"Okay, okay." He raises his hands in mock surrender. "I may have kind of asked Kyle to give us a little something to get our entrepreneurial gig started."

"Us?" I say, feeling the anger rise up. "You didn't even know I was going to sell with you until about ten minutes ago."

"What can I say, man." Tate places his hand over his heart. "I had faith."

"Whatever."

I try to stay pissed, because what he did was really out of line, but my anger fades fast. High as I am, these strong emotions are too fucking slippery to hold on to for very long.

Tate hands me a plastic packet filled with little pills, a rainbow of color. "Jesus." I know all too well exactly what this shit is. "X? You're fucking higher than I thought. We're supposed to start small, bitch. Move a little bud, see how it goes."

Tate shrugs. "We'll make more money this way. Like, I know we can sell to the girls tonight. Hell, I bet we can talk them into buying *our* hits."

He's laughing at his own ingenuity, but I ignore him. I'm too busy trying to count the pills in the packet. But being in the condition I am in, it's a bit of a challenge.

"How much is this anyway?" I ask, giving up on figuring it out for myself.

"Twenty hits," he tells me, and then he has the balls to throw another packet in my lap. "Make that forty…maybe a little more."

"You're fucking crazy. If we get caught, Tate, this isn't possession. This is possession with intent to sell."

"That's why I'm leaving the shit here with you."

"Oh, that's real fucking cool." Back to being pissed, even my high can't calm me now. I whip one of the packets back at Tate. "I am so not getting caught with forty hits of Ecstasy, asshole."

"Calm down, man." He gingerly picks up the packet I've just thrown and holds it out for me to take back. "If a cop shows up just hit the road."

"What about you?" I ask as I grudgingly accept the X.

Tate grins. "Don't worry about me. You know I can play it cool. Just swing by after the heat's gone, and we'll be back in business."

"The heat? What is this, the seventies?" I ask, laughing, but Tate's already out the door.

I tuck the two packets of Ecstasy into the back pocket of my jeans and think nothing more of it. Until a few short minutes later when a state cop pulls into the lot. Then, I panic.

I start climbing over the console to get the fuck out of there, but, suddenly, with every fiber of my being, I know I've just made the dumbest mistake of my life. That, however, doesn't stop me from slipping down into the driver's seat, throwing the car into reverse. I hit the gas, peel out of the parking lot, and leave a cloud of gravel and dust in my wake.

I've got the Focus up to eighty, music playing...loud, loud, fucking blaring. Maybe I can outrun this cocksucker? I'm tapping my hands on the steering wheel along with the beat, flying so fast it's amazing I don't lose control and crash.

But I don't, I stay steady.

I even make it a good five miles down the road before a cop heading my way—backup, I'm sure—screeches to a wide arced stop in front of me. His patrol car blocks the entire road, so I have no choice but to hit the brakes and squeal to a halt.

My car ends up parallel to the cop car, both of us straddling the lanes, engines idling like we're in some fucking action movie. The air reeks of burning rubber, and smoke billows around us. The speakers beat out a song from 50 Cent that is frankly ironic at this point.

When all the smoke clears, the sign for the lake is right smack dab in front of me. I can't help but laugh. The shit situation I'm in, and all I can think of is that Crystal and Tammy are out there, waiting, for two boys who are never going to show.

Two more cops—including the one from the store—pull up behind me. I pitch the door open, tumble from the seat. I hit the warm pavement and try to stand. Someone yells, "Hold it right there, hands on your head."

I hear guns being drawn, cocked. This isn't a movie, I know they're loaded. I squint to try to see what's happening, but all the flashing lights leave me blinded. Before I can think another drug-muddled thought, someone tackles me from behind. My face smacks right into the yellow center line, but I don't feel a fucking thing.

Whoever tackles me yanks down my hood, frisks me, and comes up with my wallet. Oh, and the forty hits of X, of course.

It's all ambient noise from that point on, but I do hear, "Chase Gartner, you're under arrest."

I have no idea that, despite the altered state I'm in, these will be the last coherent words I will remember for a very long time.

*

The time following has no sense of structure. Days, weeks, they all blend together. I'm in jail, facing a long, long list of charges. But it's the X that has me fucked.

Bond is set high. I call my mom, but all she does is cry. Like, these horrible wailing sobs that do nothing but make my head ache more than ever. She keeps apologizing for not having the money and swears she'll help me when she can. I hang up. I won't be holding my breath. The past has taught me not to put too much stock into Abby's flimsy promises. Mirages in the desert are what they are—get too close and they disappear.

My grandmother wants to mortgage the farmhouse, all the property around it. We're talking a good fifty-five acres. It'd be enough to make bail, but I tell her *no way*. She's done enough for me already, and look at how I've repaid her. I don't deserve her money…or her love.

So I'm on my own. And not thinking very clearly. Once all the illegal shit is out of my system, I find myself in a constant state of agitation. I can't sleep, I barely eat. I sweat bullets even when it feels like I'm freezing.

Eventually all that passes, but then all I want to do is fight. Like beat heads in. It's worse than when I was back in Vegas; I feel so much more fucking rage. I sit around clenching my fists, hoping for a chance to kick some poor unsuspecting soul's ass.

Finally, my wish is granted.

They throw a cellmate in with me and my ass is on him like an animal, beating the hell out of this never-saw-me-coming sap. But then two guards see what I'm doing, pull me off the bloodied and broken man, and promptly return the favor.

Another blur of pain.

This one, though, I welcome. The medical staff gives me plenty of drugs, legal ones this time. And still more before I am put before the judge.

Even in the sedated fog I float around in, I quickly learn the law…and some new math.

MDMA, Ecstasy—X, as I like to call it—is a schedule I narcotic, and carries as stiff a penalty as heroin if you're caught dealing, which they naturally assume I was. Casual users don't tote around forty-plus hits of Ecstasy, but dealers do.

I say nothing one way or the other to dispel their myth, I rat no one out. I just stay quiet and accept my fate.

My math lesson continues…

Ten pills are equal to one gram, and I've been caught with over forty pills. Forty pills equal four grams, which is more than enough to be charged with possession with intent to sell. But I already knew that part, right?

My lesson isn't over though. It's only just beginning.

I learn in Pennsylvania, the state in which I've been apprehended, four grams can easily earn you a prison sentence. This is especially true when you don't have enough money to hire a good attorney. Add to that, your public defender isn't getting paid enough to care. Not that you're doing much to help the overworked, underpaid man do his job. And, oh yeah, don't forget that one prior arrest for fighting last fall. It didn't seem like much at the time, but it sure haunts your ass now.

Are you keeping up?

Some final math…

Four grams buys you a six-year sentence at a state correctional institute when you have no resources, and, really, no heart to fight it.

Twenty years of age feels like ninety when your freedom is stripped away.

It takes one hundred and forty-three steps to walk down a long, noisy corridor to reach cell block seventy-two.

And when they turn the key, you hear one life—the only one you've ever known up until now—ending.

"It's all about the numbers, man," as Tate would say.

It sure is, my friend. It sure is.